Metaphorosis

April 2023

Beautifully made speculative fiction

Also from Metaphorosis

Metaphorosis Magazine

Metaphorosis: Best of 20xx
Metaphorosis 20xx: The Complete Stories
annual issues, from 2016

Monthly issues

Plant Based Press

Best Vegan Science Fiction & Fantasy
annual issues, 2016-2020

from B. Morris Allen:
Chambers of the Heart: speculative stories
Susurrus
Allenthology: Volume I
Tocsin: and other stories
Start with Stones: collected stories
Metaphorosis: a collection of stories

Verdage

Reading 5X5 x3: Changes
Reading 5X5 x2: Duets
Score – an SFF symphony
Reading 5X5: Readers' Edition
Reading 5X5: Writers' Edition

Vestige

The Nocturnals, by Mariah Montoya

Metaphorosis

April 2023

edited by
B. Morris Allen

ISSN: 2573-136X (online)
ISBN: 978-1-64076-255-8 (e-book)
ISBN: 978-1-64076-256-5 (paperback)

from
Metaphorosis Publishing

Neskowin

April 2023

Shortcut to Happily Ever After

Ben Wan

Dedicated to Dr. Larry Yip

"Wanna grab coffee sometime?" Daniel Woo looked across at the cute cashier with the big glasses for her reaction. Her name tag read 'STEPH'. As he watched her surprised expression form into a smile, he logged her name into his memory.

"You're awfully forward, aren't you?"

Daniel smiled back. "I just don't like wasting time."

Steph laughed. "Alright. Phone?" Daniel handed it over to her as she typed in her number. "When's your day off?" he asked.

"Tuesday."

"How 'bout next Tuesday then? Five o'clock? The place next door?"

Steph laughed. "*Wow.* You really don't waste time."

You have no idea, he thought, as he took his phone back, said good-bye, and walked out. To Steph, Daniel must have seemed incredibly confident. But had she met him months ago, she would've met a completely different man. A timid man. Because back then, he hadn't had *the watch.*

Outside, he unrolled his sleeve to reach it; his key to finding love, his shortcut to 'happily ever after', conveniently wrapped around his wrist.

He made it a habit now, when asking someone on a date, to set up a specific time and place. The women usually thought he just liked to plan. But really, it was so he'd know where to tell the watch to go. *Next Tuesday. 5PM. Place next door.* He finished with the settings, took a breath, and pushed in the dials on the watch.

In an instant, he was standing on the same street, but the cars and pedestrians had all changed around him. He still hadn't gotten used to jumping between the present and the future. It felt like skipping from chapter to chapter on a Blu-ray disc. Except he was actually *in* the movie.

He peeked into the window of the coffee shop. Sure enough, his future self and Steph were inside. *So she shows up to the first date*, he thought. *But how* well *does it go?*

He programmed the watch again and jumped forward an hour later, where he saw the two of them outside the shop. Together, they were laughing. He overheard himself set up the next date at a restaurant next week.

Daniel knew exactly where it was. He took a long walk over to it a few blocks away and programmed the watch again. This time, he watched himself and Steph walk out, nervous laughter from both of them. As they stopped by the street, there was a pause. He had to cringe just watching the awkwardness, along with the fact that for some reason, neither of them seemed to be as happy as on the previous date.

He hid, hearing his nervous future self ask, "So, uh, want a ride back?"

There was a pause and Steph awkwardly said, "Listen, Daniel...you seem like a great guy..."

He didn't need to hear more. He had heard it all before.

'We just don't seem like a fit.'

'I'm just not feeling the chemistry.'

'Maybe we could be friends.'

He watched his future self's expression change to disappointment. It was that same expression that made Daniel feel relieved. So it wouldn't work out. *No need to go on this date, then. Saved myself from getting my hopes up.*

His other self, after a minute, regained his composure and told her, "I understand. It was, uh, it was fun." As Steph walked off to her own Uber, Daniel turned away from his future disappointment and set the watch back to the present day.

Now, he was outside of the shop again, looking back through the window at Steph, who had just given out her number to him. A Steph who had no idea what he had just seen.

A few hours later, Steph got a sincere phone call from Daniel.

"I know this is gonna sound really weird," he said, "But I'm gonna have to cancel next Tuesday. It's not you, it's just…I realized I'm just not in a place to date right now."

"Oh," said Steph, who was more surprised by the sudden news than hurt. "Uhh, no problem. Thanks for not wasting time. Again."

"Of course."

"See you around the shop?"

"Sure," said Daniel. After hanging up, he sighed in relief. He always felt bad about doing this, but in the end, he knew he was dodging a bullet. Just like he had done with the others.

Steph was the third woman he had canceled on before even the first date. There were no hard feelings, especially given that none of these women had a chance to develop any attachment to him. It wasn't selfish either. He had spared all of *them* the same hurt too. The hurt he saw from simply looking into their futures. No more failed relationships. No more heartbreak. He would keep peeking into the future until he *knew* for certain that he had found a relationship that would last.

He set the phone down on his dining table. Only to jump.

There, standing in his living room, was a tall woman with a ponytail. She wore a long black coat of a snakeskin leather material. And she was pointing something that looked an awful lot like a gun at him.

"What have you been doing with that watch?!"

"What?!" Daniel put his hands up. *Oh fuck*, he thought.

He looked at the gun. It didn't look anything like the firearms he was familiar with. And then he saw it on her wrist...the same 'watch' he wore. Just in a different color.

He had wondered about the origin of the 'watch' when he found it. Now it was catching up to him.

The owner of the 'watch' was here. And she wasn't happy.

He stammered. "Okay, okay, I can explain..."

Six Months Ago...

The night Chloe left him wasn't the worst part. Sure, Daniel cried after it was all over. But it was just a couple hours until the mercy of sleep took him. Asleep, he could forget what happened. Asleep, he and Chloe would still be together...

No, the worst part of the breakup was the day after.

Because now he had an entire day to remember that she had walked out on him. He'd wake up and look across at her empty spot in bed, knowing he would never see her face there again. He had spent their entire relationship in this one bedroom apartment, yet now it felt even smaller.

It seemed like this was always something that happened to him. Ever since he was a child, he had wanted to live out the stories he grew up with, where the hero would always find love. Yet whenever he found someone special and got attached, she'd inevitably leave him. Chloe was just the latest in a series. Once again, he was left with unfulfilled dreams and fantasies. Trips they would never travel together. Movies he would never get to watch with her. Gifts he would never to give to her. The worst, of course, was the feeling of being chronically unwanted, that all he would find was rejection, heartbreak, and loneliness. And yet, there was always a part of him that hoped that he'd find someone who'd help him prove that wrong. Someone who would prove that he *was* wanted and could be loved.

Chloe had felt like that 'someone' at first, but something had been holding her back. She had admitted several times that she had trouble getting close to the guys she dated. He had hoped, or rather expected, that as he continued to show he cared, she'd see that he was different, and gradually be as intimate and vulnerable with him as he was with her.

Instead, all he did was drive her away. Maybe she was afraid he'd hurt her the same way that the other guys did. Yet the more he tried to forgive her, the more resentment he felt towards her for punishing him for the sins of her exes. *She could at least have punished me for my own sins,* he thought. *That at least would have been fair.*

The pain carried over from one day to the next.

He started burying himself at work in the morgue to distract himself. Suicides, unfortunately, spiked during the holidays. There was a common depression, triggered by a yearning to be with others and a realization, for many, that the yearning could never be fulfilled.

He looked around at the dead around him. He knew he should feel grateful to be the only one in the room breathing. But instead, he felt like he could relate to them, at least on the inside. Cold. Numb. Nothing left to care about.

1:30 came around. Daniel had heated up his lunch, a can of clam chowder that he usually packed because it was easy to microwave in the kitchen.

He took it back to his office, only for his boss to barge in.

"The cops have been asking about this John Doe for way too long. I need you to perform the autopsy *asap*."

The John Doe was a man in his forties. Nothing unusual about his appearance. But there was an ID card that was unrecognizable from any state's driver's license, giving the name John Tempest.

To everyone, it seemed fake. The police were at a loss. The fingerprints matched no database. Neither did his DNA. Nor, strangely enough, did his teeth match any dental records.

The man was a complete ghost.

Daniel performed the autopsy, as requested. It seemed that the cause of death was a heart attack. No murder or suicide. Just his heart giving out. (In a way, he could relate.)

It was about halfway through the autopsy that he remembered the clam chowder sitting back at his office. Probably cold and likely spoiled by now.

He went back to his desk and tossed out his lunch. The *thud* as the bowl hit the bottom of the trash can felt satisfying, but it wasn't enough to quell the anger he felt.

Now he'd have to wait until dinner to eat. Which pissed him off further. Work was supposed to be his distraction. But now it had become such a distraction that he was skipping lunch. And skipping lunch would just remind him of Chloe and how she always packed lunch for him... and well, work wasn't such a distraction anymore now, was it?

Towards the end of his shift, he looked through the belongings that were found on 'John Tempest'. Perhaps he could help the police find a clue to the man's identity.

Among the belongings was a watch. It didn't match any brand that Daniel had been familiar with. Instead of a single dial to adjust the time and the date, there were multiple ones. There even seemed to be ones to adjust the month and the year, which made it even more unusual.

Daniel played with one of the dials absentmindedly. *It seems like a good watch*, he thought as he turned the hand back a few hours.

Lost in thought, he snapped the dial back in. That was when he felt *the jump*.

He was still in his office. But his surroundings felt...different.

Because the clam chowder was now back to sitting on his desk. Still warm, steam rising from it.

That was strange, he thought. How could that be back there? He hadn't had it out since lunch time, which was...

He looked at the dead man's watch. Sure enough, it had been set to lunch hour. *1:30PM.*

There was no way. Or was there?

His mind must be playing tricks on him. And yet, here was the soup, as it would have sat. But if he had really gone back, where was his past self? He snuck out into the hallway, towards the lab, took a peek in the window...

And *there he was.* Performing the autopsy on the dead body, forgetting all about his lunch back in the office.

He had traveled in time.

Which likely then explained John Tempest. Tempest. As in *Tempus*. As in *time*.

The man was a time traveler. A *dead* time traveler. He wouldn't have any record. Was he from the past? The future? A different world entirely?

Daniel didn't know. All he wanted to learn about now was the watch.

He turned the dial and adjusted it a few hours further back. Then a few hours forward. Each time, he kept adjusting, spying on his past self in the lab or office, and testing the watch further. *Shit, what time was it when I first started jumping around?* he wondered. He needed to go back to his present time. His *real* time. He remembered it being towards the end of his shift and estimated that it must have been around 5:30. He set the watch and jumped once again, finding himself back in his office at the end of the day. The clam chowder was gone and John Tempest's belongings were all on his desk. He had returned to the present. Daniel wasn't sure whether to sigh in relief or cheer in excitement. It *worked.*

What now? Anyone he reported this to would think he was crazy, until he demonstrated it. But then they'd surely take it away. Examine its functions. Use it for their own purposes. No, he had a unique opportunity here.

John Tempest, whoever he was, seemed to have used this watch for time travel. So far, Daniel could only move through time in the same spot. Which probably meant that if he wanted to go back in time to watch the Beatles debut on the Ed Sullivan Show, he'd have to physically *go* to the Ed Sullivan Theater in New York in the present before setting anything.

Tempest had wound up in this timeline where he died. He certainly wasn't using it anymore. So if Daniel took the watch... who would miss it?

Plus, who would even find out? The police might have a record of the watch's existence, but with other cases preoccupying them, they probably wouldn't notice if he kept it to himself. And considering that Tempest probably wasn't even from this time period, the police would never find any leads about him.

It was settled, then. He was going to keep it. But what would he do with it? It didn't take him long to think about it. He knew deep down what he wanted...

He was going to use it to find the love of his life.

At first, he was tempted to go back and undo the breakup with Chloe. But what exactly would he undo? Would he even be able to convince her to stay with him? If he couldn't, he'd just be opening up an old wound. He wanted to make himself feel *better*, not worse.

No, he'd only use the watch to take peeks into the future and come back, rather than change his past. And this time, the watch could help him know that he was moving on with the *right* person, rather than wasting any more time with the *wrong* person.

So Daniel started putting himself out there.

First, he met Ann at a party through his co-worker Simon. "You're not seeing anyone. She's not seeing anyone. I'll set you guys up," he told Daniel.

"Why don't you go for her?"

"Already tried," said Simon. "But she goes for nice guys."

Daniel shook his head. That was a backhanded compliment if he knew it. But he was intrigued.

Simon gestured him over. "Hey, Ann. Meet my buddy, Daniel."

Daniel looked over at a cute girl in a leather jacket. Okay, he wasn't hating this experience so far.

"Hey Daniel," said Ann.

"Alright, you two talk. I'm out."

Daniel watched Simon go. Ann said, "Well that wasn't an awkward introduction at all."

"Not at all," he agreed. "So how do you know Simon? Other than him trying to hit on you?"

She laughed. "Is that what he said he did?"

"Clearly he wasn't that successful."

"I'm friends with his roommate. We met that way, unfortunately."

Daniel nodded. He could tell that she was wondering what his connection was. "Well, I work with Simon," he said.

"With the dead people."

"Yep, with the dead people. Which kinda sucks, actually. Because I thought that meant I wouldn't have to deal with anyone annoying. But then I met him."

She laughed. Once they hit it off about classic literature, she gave him her number and he decided to take the watch for a spin.

The planning was simple. He'd make it a habit of scheduling each new date at the end of the previous one. As an observer, he'd bounce around and spy on how the date went. Then, he'd overhear his future self set up the next time and know exactly where and when to pop up.

After calling Ann to schedule a meeting at a local bookstore, he used the watch to jump to the first date. Then the second. The third. Then months of dating until the night he asked her to be his girlfriend.

Daniel had been tempted to stop peeking then, already satisfied with the future. But he didn't just want another relationship. He wanted *the* relationship. The last relationship he'd ever be in. He wanted to know the *whole* future. So he watched Cliff Notes of an entire relationship unfold. Their first time meeting the parents. Their first fight.

And then, after a year of dating, the breakup. Another girl out of the blue who would leave and break his heart.

And once again, he'd find himself alone in a one bedroom apartment that was starting to feel even smaller.

He wound the watch back to the day after the party when they first met. Then he called Ann, telling her that he'd have to cancel their date at the bookstore and that he just wasn't really in a good place to see anyone. Maybe he'd just see her at another of his friend's parties again and save her from Simon trying to shoot his shot a second time. She found his honesty refreshing and genuinely wished him luck.

There was a wave of relief in what he had done, not to mention pride. He hadn't wasted Ann's time and she hadn't wasted his. They could move on to the right people without baggage. He felt ready to use the watch again on the next girl he met.

That was Kristine.

They had matched online. Daniel wasn't really a fan of online dating and trying to make conversations on the apps. But, as a change, Kristine had started the conversation first.

She seemed like the opposite of Ann. For one thing, she wasn't a book nerd at all. For another, she was less sarcastic and more direct in her interest. The day after they started talking, she was already messaging him, 'Hey, handsome', and before he could float the idea by her first, she was the one proposing, 'Wanna get drinks this week?'

Still, Daniel wanted to see what would happen. So once again he used the watch to skip forward.

A couple of dates in, he saw that he'd invited her to his place. They both seemed to like cooking and he had wanted to show off his pasta maker. Though for some reason, it wasn't in its usual place and he'd had to buy a new one. That was odd. He could have sworn that he always kept it in the same spot in the same cabinet.

He knew this relationship would last longer than the previous one once he saw that, two years in, he and Kristine were still together.

Then eventually, engaged.

But he just kept pushing and jumping forward. Would she marry him? He had to *know*. Even when the wedding was already planned, a date set, invites sent out...he felt that he needed the confirmation. He needed to see himself married before he'd go on that date.

So it was discouraging, but not at all surprising that, when he jumped forward, he saw Kristine call off the engagement.

He overheard himself from the other room, asking, "What did I do?"

Kristine replied, "I just feel like...you don't put in any effort with me anymore."

At that point, Daniel stopped listening. He couldn't stand the sound of his own future voice breaking and crying. And he couldn't stand to keep watching Kristine break his heart even further.

If he was feeling that from just witnessing everything, he could only imagine what it'd be like to *live* it. And it made him even more grateful. This watch from John Tempest was a gift that spared him from pain.

He didn't even want to hear the rest of the argument or wait until Kristine had left. He knew her well enough, at least from observing their relationship, that she wouldn't change her mind.

And he'd be alone, once again, in a studio apartment that was still feeling smaller.

Better to just go back in time and end it. He reset the watch so the sound of his crying in the background would stop.

A month later, he went into the shop and met Steph.

The Present

Daniel finished his story. The woman with the gun had settled in at his dining table, drinking coffee that he had brewed for her. She had put the weapon down too, though the barrel was still pointed in his general direction.

She sipped the coffee in silence, thinking over Daniel's story. He cleared his throat.

"So...you must have known John Tempest, then. Miss...?"

She set down the cup, staring down at it and seeming to ignore him until she finally answered.

"Call me the Overseer."

"Overseer...so what, is that a title or something? For, like, time travelers?"

"Something like that. We're the ones assigned to stop the time ripples."

"Time ripples?"

Then, as if on cue, the coffee cup disappeared from the table.

It wasn't a magic trick. But it felt like one. Almost as if something had just *edited* a jump cut from a movie into reality. Even stranger, the Overseer had looked satisfied, almost having expected it to happen.

Daniel sat up, alarmed. "What...What just happened? What the hell is this?"

"Like I said. Time ripple." She stood up. "Mr. Woo, I tracked you down because your apartment appears to be the center of a set of time ripples."

"What are those? Some kind of butterfly effect?"

"In a way. When time gets undone, your environment changes around you. Usually, you don't even notice the changes. They usually start with your living arrangements..."

Daniel thought it through. He'd been living in a studio apartment for the last six years...but had it always been a studio?

Hadn't he been in a *one bedroom* apartment at some point? Or had he just dreamed or imagined that? No, that couldn't be right. Was she causing him to remember new things or was she causing him to *think* he was remembering new things?

She continued. "Then, certain things go missing. It's probably happened to you before. You can't find something. You don't know where you put it. And if it's not where you last put it, you chalk it up to a bad memory. But it's not. It's actually the beginning of a time ripple."

Things go missing...like a pasta maker? he thought.

"Because for just a few moments in time, whatever's missing actually *stopped existing*. You get residual memories of something that's no longer there and the mind just rationalizes that it's lost or misplaced. Until you stop remembering that it actually existed at all."

Daniel looked alarmed. The Overseer noticed. "Don't worry. Sometimes, what's lost gets found. Sure, it's not where you remember it. But you're so happy you found it again, you don't really question how it got there. You chalk it up to bad memory or just being forgetful. But you didn't forget. Time just set itself right again. And it took an Overseer to bring it back."

Daniel thought of all the times he had found something that he had once lost and how it never seemed to be in the last place he remembered. Just how common were these time ripples?

"Your...dating adventures are responsible for the time ripples in this sector. To put it mildly, you undid things that shouldn't have been undone. And time is making us all pay the consequences. So here's what we'll do, kid. You're gonna return that to me. That's Overseer property."

She grabbed his wrist, undoing the clasp on the watch without letting him object. "Next, you're gonna fix the mess you created."

"How?"

"All those women you turned down. You have to go back and date them. In *real* time."

Daniel froze. That had to be a joke. "But... But I know the future. That'd just be a waste of time."

"Would it?"

"I spent like two years with one of them! I know how it ends!"

"Do you?"

"Can you stop asking me questions?!"

She shot him a glare. "Something that was supposed to happen never happened. That's the cause of this. To fix it, you have to *make* those events happen. Everyone you were supposed to date. You have to *date* them. That's the only way this works."

Daniel could sense the judgment in her tone. He tried to think of another way to get out of this. "I'd be wasting years of my life!" he argued.

"You'd be saving life as we know it. Sounds dramatic, I know, but I'm not wrong. If we don't stop the ripples, all of us are eventually gonna disappear. Like that coffee cup. Which you're gonna forget, by the way, after we're done with this conversation. So you can either do this and make it right or I have to do something drastic."

"Like what?"

She tapped on her gun. "Like go back to when you got the watch and erase you from this timeline." Daniel blinked, speechless. "Not up for that? Didn't think so," she said.

And with that, the Overseer set the dials on her own watch, then grabbed his hand.

Their surroundings snapped into place in an instant. They were back at his room as it had been months ago. "Here we are," she said.

Daniel looked outside. It had gone from day to night. Two dogs were in the middle of a barking match with each other while their owners were trying to restrain them. "So wait, where am *I*? Like, where's the old me?"

"You've set up a date with Ann and now you've gone forward in time to see if you two have a future. But instead of you coming back to cancel on her, we're just gonna branch off into a new timeline from here. One where you actually date Ann. You know, like a normal person."

The Overseer clicked her watch. The barking outside stopped. Daniel peeked out. The dogs and their owners were completely frozen.

"If it doesn't work with her, then we go onto Kristine. And then Steph. Until you experience everything you were supposed to experience. Text Ann to reconfirm you're still going out. Time will resume and the new timeline will begin."

"But I'm undoing what I actually lived through. Doesn't that create, like, another paradox? If I didn't live through turning down these women, how would I still exist to do this?"

"Doesn't work that way," said the Overseer. "As long as these *new* paradoxes fulfill what was supposed to happen, time will fix itself. You know how a string gets tangled and knotted?"

"Yeah?"

"There's always that grace period where you can still untangle it. Before it gets too much. That's where we're at, kid. Right before the point of no return. The point where we can still untangle the string."

The Overseer took his phone and pulled up Ann's number, then handed it back to him.

"So do it," she said. "Untangle it."

Daniel stood by the front door of the bookstore, waiting on his first date, his *real* first date, with Ann. It occurred to him that he might have watched this date before, but it wasn't actually him who had gone through it.

What if he said something stupid and he never got into a relationship with her in the first place? He remembered seeing his heartbroken self back on the couch, feeling the way he had felt after Chloe left. Yes, maybe he'd actually prefer to just screw it all up now. It'd be a quicker way to get to the next person. Finish the mission for the Overseer. Correct his mistake. Get out of this mess.

Then Ann walked in and the plan went out the window.

For Ann, it had just been a few days ago since she met Daniel, but for him, it had been *months*.

He forgot how much he had liked looking in her eyes at the party and the way she had made him feel the first time that he met her.

Their first date, time-wise, lasted about twelve hours.

But neither he nor Ann really felt time go by. She spent the night at his place, which was something he hadn't predicted, since he hadn't stuck around long enough to find out the first time he watched. Other than the embarrassment of not having a clean coffee cup for her in the morning (and feeling like it was weird that he had so few in the first place), it was the perfect first date.

After she left his place, he got to thinking. Yes, he knew the future. Yes, he had seen that in a year from now, it wouldn't work out. But...couldn't he just enjoy being around her for now? Couldn't he just enjoy not being lonely and broken up over Chloe again?

So he kept seeing her. A couple dates in and she was all he could think about. Whenever she texted, he'd always smile and text back as soon as he could. Eventually, she was *constantly* texting him. Maybe she was getting clingy, but since he liked her already, he didn't mind. He *wanted* to text her all day. It was refreshing to not have to fight for someone's attention, the way he always had to with Chloe.

A few months in, he asked her to be his girlfriend. A month after that, they took their first trip together. But as the relationship grew, so did the fear.

Because he knew the future. He knew this relationship was doomed. That she was going to hurt him in the end. He tried to brush it aside and convince himself he was too in love right now to care.

But that love was starting to deteriorate. Whenever they'd argue, even over something small like what type of onions to buy at the grocery store, it was another nail in the coffin. *Is this why she's gonna leave?* he thought.

And yet whenever she said something nice or gave him a surprise gift or comforted him when he had a bad day, he couldn't really believe her either, even though he wanted to. She'd say, "I love you," and he'd wonder, *Do you really? You won't in a couple of months.*

Soon their one-year anniversary was approaching and the anxiety was taking over him. Ann would be leaving any day now. She'd drop him just like Chloe had. He'd go back to crying himself to sleep, waking up next to an empty space in the bed, and sleepwalking from day to day.

He knew what he had to do. And he didn't like it.

When he came over to her place the next night, he told her that it was over. That he felt like he didn't see a future anymore with her. He said it very matter-of-fact. After all, he thought, she was on the same page "You've probably been feeling this too anyway," he said.

But when he looked in her eyes, all he saw was hurt and confusion. She stammered, "No, I...I haven't been feeling that way at all." Daniel stared back with the same confusion. "But I thought...I saw..."

"You saw what, Daniel?"

What could he possibly tell her? That he had time traveled? He'd sound insane. And yet somehow, in knowing how it was going to end, he had acted so differently that he had changed the outcome and the timeline itself. Worse, after all these months of hating Chloe, now he felt like he *was* Chloe. He felt a sense of *loathing* towards himself for putting someone through what he had experienced. Chloe had left him out of fear of getting hurt and ended up hurting him instead. And now he was about to do the same thing to a sweet girl he loved who didn't deserve it.

"Okay, look, I'm sorry, I didn't mean what I said. I've just been confused." He reached out for her hand. He had to fix this.

But she turned away. "You don't know what you want, Daniel. That's the problem."

"No, that's not true."

"It *is* true. You say you want to be with me, but half the time, your mind's somewhere else. Whatever I try, it's not enough. So maybe you're right. Maybe we should just end this."

"I'm sorry, I—I didn't mean for it to be like this."

"Just go." She kept herself turned away and waited. Daniel couldn't think of anything else to do but comply. She hadn't shown much emotion, but when he walked out, he could hear her crying on the other side of the door.

He wasn't anything special. Just part of a vicious cycle. Hearts were broken. Heartbroken people went off to break other hearts. And it would continue over and over and over again. He had to stop it. He gave Ann a couple days of space before calling her.

Except when he called, the voice of an old man picked up on the other end. "Johnson Residence."

No. Daniel immediately hung up. He searched for Ann on social media. All her accounts were gone. He had hoped that she had just blocked him, but why would she have changed her number?

Then he visited her apartment building to check the register. There was a different name in her unit. She couldn't have moved out in just *two days* just because of him. He hoped she did because the alternative was much worse. At work, he approached Simon to see if he was right. "Ann and I broke up."

"Ann?"

"Yeah. You know, my girlfriend. The one you introduced me to at a party..."

"You had a girlfriend?"

Daniel ran off. He needed answers. Sure enough, when he was alone, the Overseer appeared.

"I warned you," she said. "The world's population just dropped by 1 million and nobody noticed except you."

"But how do I still remember?"

"You're a time traveler. Your memories linger longer than others. But you'll still forget eventually. Like that coffee cup."

"What coffee cup?"

"Exactly. Or your pasta maker."

"What pasta — never mind. If I keep going with the plan, do these people come back?"

"It's still possible, but you can't waste any more time. You still have to date the other two women."

"Wait," said Daniel. But the Overseer had already taken his phone. "On to Kristine."

"How? I only met her because I never went out with Ann."

"Not a problem," said the Overseer.

"She might not even exist now!"

But the Overseer went into the dating apps and started randomly swiping on the women. After a few matches, she handed the phone over to him.

"That should do it. Scroll through. One of them's her." She said with confidence.

Daniel looked through his matches. Sure enough, Kristine's profile was in the queue.

"How did you—?"

"Like I said, your relationships were events that *had* to happen. No matter what, Kristine would still end up matching with you on these apps."

Daniel set the phone down, shaking his head. "I just had a breakup."

"Sorry," said the Overseer. "But you don't have time. None of us do."

So Daniel reluctantly started talking to Kristine. This time, *he* started the conversation. He didn't remember exactly what he had said to her when they first talked, but he had the gist of it. He thought about the future with her he had seen. How they had almost gotten married, if he hadn't screwed it all up.

He remembered the words that she had told him. 'You don't put in any effort with me.' Maybe he would just do the opposite of what he'd seen. Maybe that would give him a different result. Put in effort.

In a way, he'd be making up for what he had just done to Ann.

So this time Daniel was the one to ask Kristine for drinks next week.

Soon enough, they were dating and he had her over for cooking dinner, so he could show off this new pasta maker he had bought, though he had no idea how to use it. (And he couldn't help shake the nagging feeling that he was *supposed* to know how to use it).

Kristine was already different from Ann. For one thing, she wasn't as quick to open up. In fact, for some time, it still felt as if he hardly knew her at all. He knew what she did for a living, of course. Her general interests. How many siblings she had. What she liked in bed.

Maybe he just needed to give it time. So he did everything he could to be a great boyfriend. He went all out on her birthday. Made sure to befriend all her friends. Gave her all his attention when she was with him.

So why was it that every time he did something nice for her, she'd always seem to run away? She'd thank him in the moment, sure, but then, she'd retreat into work and barely talk to him for a week. Naturally, this just made him push harder. He'd text her more to ask how her day went. He'd offer to cook for her more often. *Anything* to avoid being accused of not 'putting in the effort'.

Which was why it shocked him, four months into the relationship, when she said, "I don't think this is working for me."

No. No, this isn't right, he thought. *We aren't even close to the time that we broke up.*

Daniel wondered if maybe he had missed an initial breakup from his travels and the two of them would get together again after this.

But he knew that was just wishful thinking. It was the way she had said, 'I don't think this is working for me'. It was the same tone he had heard when she called off the wedding.

All he could muster in response was one word: "Why?" As in, why was this over, out of nowhere, *again*? Why couldn't he just make something work? Why was nothing he did good enough for her (or for Chloe for that matter)? *Why?*

And Kristine simply responded, "I just feel like you're too…clingy for me."

The first time, he hadn't made enough effort with Kristine. Now he had made *too* much. Maybe Kristine had just never really wanted him. Maybe she was destined to make an excuse to leave.

Maybe it wasn't even Kristine. Maybe it was just his luck in general with love. Maybe he'd always be disappointed and never find the right person.

And the Overseer returned again. This time, Daniel had nothing to share. He simply asked, "Those ripples still happening?" She nodded. Before she could elaborate, Daniel cut her off. He didn't care anymore. "Let's just get this over with."

There was one woman left: Steph.

"Lucky for you, she hasn't been rippled out of existence yet. I checked. You still have a shot at fixing this," said the Overseer. She looked like she was about to leave, but she stopped. Perhaps there was sympathy in her step. "Good luck." And with that, she was gone. It occurred to Daniel that if he pulled this off, he might never see the Overseer again.

With Ann and Kristine, he had tried to go against what he had seen. Now, what would his strategy be?

This time, there'd be no strategy. And maybe that, in itself, was a strategy. Maybe he just needed to act as if he *didn't* know the future. A part of him hoped that meant this would work out. Another part of him told him to stop being an idiot in getting his hopes up.

If the Overseer had been right about these relationships being destined to happen, then Steph would still be working at the shop now.

So he drove over and walked in. Sure enough, there she was at the cash register. He almost didn't recognize her at first without the big glasses. She must've been wearing contacts today. She wore her hair tied back and her outfit was different from what he remembered, but he figured he could have the same conversation. That was going to be the easy part.

As expected, she agreed to get coffee with him. Like before, he asked when she was off work. And like before, he scheduled it for her day off. So he arrived on that Tuesday. 5PM. The coffee shop next to the place that she worked at. And the two of them talked.

They talked for six *hours*, to the point that the place closed before they were done.

Daniel was surprised by Steph at first. It had been maybe even a year at this point since he had *actually* met her for the first time. She seemed *funnier* than he had remembered. Was she actually funnier? Or did he just *get* her humor better? And did he also find her more attractive now than before because of it?

"You know, it seems weird," she said, "But the other day when you came into the shop, I felt like I almost knew you from before."

Daniel laughed. "Really?"

"Yeah, I don't know. You just seemed so…familiar. Or I seemed familiar to you. Like did we go to school together or something?"

"I'm a SoCal boy and you're from the East Coast. I doubt it."

"I know, but still! I don't know, you just seemed like…someone I've already known for awhile. Like, you *knew* I'd say yes to coffee. Like you expected it."

Daniel just shrugged. She wasn't completely wrong. "Well I didn't know for sure. But I figured I didn't have anything to lose."

"See, a lot of people say that. But most of them don't actually act like it," she said, "What's your secret?"

He shrugged. "I'd say, learn not to expect anything."

"That's it? So you just expect to be disappointed and let yourself be surprised."

"No, expecting to be disappointed is different from not expecting anything. Because if you expect to be disappointed, you're still expecting. Which is the problem." Daniel hardly recognized what was coming out of his mouth. It felt like he was making shit up as he went along and it just happened to sound profound.

But Steph smiled and said, "I like that."

Hell, maybe it was *profound, then.* He continued, "I mean, it's basically what they say. Hope for the best, prepare for the worst…"

He'd have to put that mentality to the test soon. Because later that night, Steph agreed to go on a second date.

And in another life, it was the second date that was also their last date.

Daniel had figured that the outcome would be different from before. But whether that would be better or worse, he'd have to see.

He went into the date half excited and half feeling like a prisoner due for execution. About thirty minutes into it, she said. "I have something to confess."

Uh oh, he thought. A part of him wondered if this would be when she'd end it. Which would be really awkward, since the food hadn't even come yet.

What she actually said, however, was very different: "I just got out of a relationship like a month ago."

"Wow," he said. Then without thinking, "Me too."

"Really?! Oh my God, I totally thought I'd scare you off."

Daniel laughed. *On the contrary...*

Questions then swirled in his brain. "So that day I asked you out to coffee... what made you say 'yes' then? I mean you could've just said that you were still recovering from the last relationship. I would've gotten it..."

"Yeah, well, breakups suck. But there's no use punishing the next guy about it, is there?"

Jesus, where were you three relationships ago? Daniel thought as he took a second to collect his response. "No...no, definitely not."

He was starting to feel something for the first time. Was it comfort? No, that wasn't it. Maybe it was *desire*, but not in the sexual sense of desiring her (though he wasn't opposed to that either). It was almost a desire to open up. To share again. To just be vulnerable.

He continued talking, "You know, if I'm being frank, there's a part of me that almost didn't ask you out. Not because of you, I mean, but because I guess I was just getting jaded from the whole experience."

"Yeah, I get you. It's hard not to get hurt doing all this."

Daniel leaned forward with interest. "What helps you just put yourself out there then?"

Steph let out a breath and thought about it. "Knowing it's worse if I don't."

"And you're not afraid of getting hurt again?"

"Oh, all the time," she said, "But if I let that stop me, I'm never gonna find it, am I?"

"I guess you're right."

"How about you? What keeps you going?"

Daniel thought about how he should phrase it. Then said, "Same as you, I guess. Faith."

Steph raised a glass. "To faith, then."

They toasted and kept talking through the rest of their dinner, but Steph's attitude stuck out in his mind. Here he had been, using a stolen time traveler's watch to avoid getting hurt, while Steph had done the complete opposite. No time travel, no peeks or knowledge of how things would turn out. Just complete faith that at some point, someone was going to make all the heartache worth it.

He paid the bill, of course, and as they walked out, Daniel could feel his heart pounding.

Here it is. The moment she turns me down.

He had *really* started to like her already. He hoped things would turn out differently this time, but he felt an odd sense of calmness as he walked next to her.

He had seen this play out from the outside. The hesitation. The potential preamble on how he *seemed* like a great guy *but...*

But nothing. He had been wrong before. Maybe he'd be wrong again. He wouldn't know unless he went for it.

"So...want a ride back?" he asked. The same question he had heard himself ask in the other timeline. He noticed it came out differently from what he remembered. When he had heard himself say it originally, it felt very tentative, as if he weren't really sure if she would say yes. Here, it seemed casual. Indifferent. Almost as if he had asked her to pass the salt.

It wasn't that he needed her to say 'yes' anymore.

It was that he'd be fine if she said 'no'. That no matter what answer she gave him...he'd be okay.

He stopped, waiting for her answer. She smiled.

"A ride? Sure."

Somewhere, in a kitchen across town, a coffee cup and a pasta maker reappeared, as if they had been there all along.

A girl named Ann was back in her apartment, pouring over a book.

And Daniel was walking Steph back to his car for a ride home.

He smiled. For once, he had no idea what was going to happen next.

See Ben Wan's story "Shortcut to Happily Ever After" online at Metaphorosis.
If you liked it, leave a comment. Authors love that!
Remember to subscribe to our e-mail updates so you'll know when new stories are posted.

About the story

Unsurprisingly, the idea for "Shortcut to Happily Ever After" came to me when my last relationship ended and I found myself back in the dating pool. As I was meeting new people, I wondered how much easier it would be if, for every person we met, we could just jump forward in time to see if it would work out. If it didn't, we could call it all off before the first date, sparing everyone from future heartache. On top of that, in another job, I coach people who are inexperienced in dating and are often terrified of potential rejection. It seems almost universal that we're scared of future pain. Yet risking that pain and putting ourselves out there is necessary, both in developing ourselves and in finding a relationship that lasts. The more we try to avoid that pain, like Daniel in this story, the more we hurt that development and hold ourselves back from getting what we want.

If there are any Doctor Who fans among the readers, they might be interested to learn that this was originally conceived to be part of the Doctor Who universe. I had written a one page proposal for Big Finish's Paul Spragg Memorial Short Trips Opportunity, pitching this as an audio drama. But when another story was chosen, I still wanted to explore this premise and write it out as an original novella or short story. The Doctor wasn't the protagonist anyway, Daniel was. So I eliminated all of the Doctor Who elements and created my own world as well as my own time travel rules before I started outlining what would become "Shortcut to Happily Ever After".

When I tell people about this story, the easiest way to describe it is as a 'time travel romance'. The funny thing is that it's not really accurate. There's time travel but most of the drama happens chronologically in the present day. It's also not really a romance since it doesn't revolve around two people falling in love. It instead revolves around one hurt individual who learns to face his fears in dating and grow from it. I hope this story speaks to people going through that same journey and inspires them to face their fears as well.

A question for the author

Q: Do you write with a particular audience in mind?

A: At the risk of sounding self-centered, the first audience I write for is myself! If I'm not actually interested in the premise or I'm bored at any point with the story, then my audience is going to feel the same way. I want whatever I write to be something that I'd not just read, but reread over and over again from how much I connect to it. I think about how I would get invested in a story and find a way to channel that for the reader. That said, I don't want to be self indulgent and only write for an audience of one. I want people to relate to it. To balance that out, I tend to write about a particular theme or experience that most would find relatable, but in a way that feels interesting or unique.

Storytelling connects us and helps us feel less alone. Whatever my protagonist is dealing with, there's a high chance other people have dealt with it too. In the case of "Shortcut to Happily Ever After", I channeled my own emotions about getting back into dating after a breakup, knowing that others have felt the same way, like the heartache over their last relationship or feeling jaded with their current options. Some might connect with the story after going through their own heartbreak. Others might feel inspired to get back into dating again. If even one person says this story helps them cope with their own dating experiences, then I've done my job.

About the author

Ben Wan is a cancer survivor who's been making the most out of his second chance at life. Aside from writing, he's a former musician who's performed in Carnegie Hall, a black belt in Kung Fu San Soo, and a coach for Become Sharp in helping introverted clients succeed with dating, confidence, and social skills. He's currently the co-host and "Man Who Knows Too Much About Batman" for the podcast *Superhero Stuff You Should Know*, where his cat Alfie makes cameo appearances.

www.benwanwriter.com, @SuperHousePod

Trapped in Memory

Dan Le Fever

"Touchdown in T-minus fifteen," a crackling voice said over the comm channel.

Pilot Kehvan-30 toggled that the message was received as he prepared to do his part in landing *Last Train* and the three million sleeping colonists aboard. After nearly a thousand years, they had finally arrived at the new planet where humanity would once again thrive after the destruction of the planet Earth.

Through the Translink System implanted in each crewmember, Kehvan had perfect recall of the day the Moon had crashed into Earth's surface . Yet he felt nothing when he watched the memory vid recorded by Kehvan-01, his genetic line's first iteration. And why would he? Earth had never been his home, though he replayed the vid daily as a reminder of his purpose. As one of the seventeen distinct Pilots aboard *Last Train*, his only desire was to land safely.

"T-minus twelve."

He turned his attention to the screen on the wall in front of him. The atmosphere of the world they approached had a red hue, and the information that scrolled across the screen matched what the ancient scientists had predicted: oxygen, carbon, and nitrogen were all within acceptable parameters to support life.

For a split second, Kehvan wondered what it would be like to walk on the surface. To smell unrecycled air, feel the warmth of sunlight, or taste fresh food grown from the soil. Then the nano-wires of the Translink chip that spiderwebbed throughout his body took over and made him focus once more on the controls. He chastised himself for letting his mind wander and blamed the ripvids he had watched before his duty activation. Unlike memory vids, these had been pulled by

Pilot Seyra-01 from Earth's satellites before they ceased transmitting. Later, watching them became a minor act of rebellion as she learned how to share them with other crewmembers. They were not outright banned, but generations of Captains had restricted viewing to those on downshift.

Seyra-30 had talked about it with him once, why the ripvids were such a big deal. It was basic psychology. "My guess, scientists didn't know how we'd react if we got it in our heads that our lives were a complete waste. Probably figured we'd walk out an airlock just because we can't pet a dog, walk on a beach, or get fat. I don't know if my life is missing anything, but that's probably because we've always had a purpose. Especially *our* iteration. We're marked for Landing."

Seyra spoke in a peculiar accent that she had picked up from one such vid and Kehvan, who slept beneath her bunk, often heard her practicing it when she thought no one else was awake. Best described as sparse, their quarters were in a narrow room, with rows of beds on one wall and a communal bathroom with showers and toilets. A few days ago, one of the waste reclaimers had malfunctioned and sprayed urine from one of the pipes. He could remember how upset she had been after they smelled like urine for their entire shift.

"We piss down one hole just to have it rain on us from another," she had grumbled.

"It's been a thousand years," he had said to her. "Things are bound to break down."

"T-minus eight."

He shook his head to clear his thoughts and activated the stimneedle in his arm. The chemicals would keep him hyper-focused as he and the other Pilots landed the massive ship. *Last Train* was enormous, far larger than even some of the cities of old Earth. The ancient scientists had not wanted to put all their trust in computers, so, by design, the ship required a small army of seventeen individually produced Pilots to keep her from tearing apart when she entered the planet's atmosphere.

As the stim took hold, his heart thrummed in rhythm with the powerful engines, and he pressed the button indicating his readiness. Across the ship, each Pilot did the same. Seyra was the last to signal before they broke through the cloud barrier and the ship began to shake. Gritting his teeth, Kehvan held the control sticks tightly while all Pilots worked in tandem to keep *Last Train* level.

"The dream of every colonist is to wake up on the surface. That dream rests now on your shoulders," the Captain had said during her speech right before they began the landing preparations. It had been a good speech.

Chosen from the previous generation of Pilots, the Captain had served fifty-five rotations since her decantation, which made her the oldest crewmember aboard *Last Train*. She was a woman of firm convictions that wanted nothing more than to see them fulfill their task of shepherding Earth's survivors to their new home. She also happened to be Seyra-29, which was probably why Seyra-30's minor infractions were often overlooked.

Also, Seyra-30 was skilled at keeping the major ones from being noticed.

For instance, right after the Captain's speech, Seyra had done something odd by taking his hand. Contact among the crew was not necessarily forbidden, just highly irregular. Pulling him aside as the others filed out of the conference room, she had asked him what he looked forward to the most after they landed.

"To see the sky," he answered, which every Kehvan had wanted since his first iteration.

Usually, that was the end of the conversation, but this time, she said, "Promise me you'll wait and see it with me." It was a simple enough request, so he agreed, and her face lit up in a way he had never seen before. But as he was about to inquire why, the Captain had ordered them to their posts.

"T-minus three," the Captain said now over the comm. "Landing imminent. Release."

As he had been trained, Kehvan initiated the reverse thrusters and deployed the landing struts before taking up the sticks again. Everything was nominal until an alarm blared in the cramped room. The green lights along the console flickered to red all at once, and he knew that something had gone catastrophically wrong.

Partially deafened by the siren, Kehvan heard a faint shout from the comm speaker, "Pull up!"

Kehvan slipped on his headset to request confirmation just as the Captain's voice came through. "Negative. Gravity too strong. It'll tear us apart."

"The damn ground's about to do the same in a minute," Seyra argued, and Kehvan realized she'd been the one to tell them to pull up. He didn't have time to think about how that was possible; the on-screen readout indicated they had only seconds left before touchdown.

Since his decantation, Kehvan had looked forward to feeling *Last Train* touch down, but now he wished for anything else. The ship shuddered violently as all the Pilots continued their descent. All that is, except for Seyra, who had powered the thrusters of her section to ascend again, throwing off the ship's approach angle. Kehvan wanted to shout at her to think of the colonists, but he did not dare take his hands off the sticks to reach for the comm. Then the ship clipped the ground at landing speed, and his head smashed into the control panel.

From within the void, something rang every few seconds. Kehvan lifted a hand and was surprised he could see it in the perfect nothingness. The ringing came again, closer this time. Out beyond his consciousness, he saw a red glow each time it sounded. Willing himself forward, he made his way in that direction. The ring grew louder with each step until it shook his whole body. Finally reaching the glow, he saw a telephone. Strange, he thought. He'd never seen one in person. Kehvan picked up the receiver, as people often did in the ripvids, and asked, "Hello?"

Pain wracked his body as he came to. Bright lights flashed in his vision. At first, he thought it was his eyes, but as he blinked to clear them, he saw sparks cascading down the walls from cracked bulkheads. Twisted conduits and exposed wires were everywhere. Coughing as he breathed in the scent of burning ozone, he assessed his situation. Though he was sprawled on the control panel, he was still miraculously strapped in his chair, with the telephone ringing in his left ear. As he started to question how it had followed him out of the void, he realized what he was actually hearing was the emergency comm channel.

He tried to hit the receive button, but cold agony tore through his left arm. Gasping in pain, Kehvan tested his right hand and found it hurt significantly less. He pushed back from the panel and took in a few labored breaths. There was a moment when he thought his chest had been caved in, but he reminded himself that he was still alive, so it couldn't be that serious. Aside from the occasional flash of sparks, the only lights he had to go by were from a few buttons on the controls and one of the vidscreens that randomly flickered green.

By the odd angle his left arm hung in his lap, he deduced it was broken. He tasted blood. But clearly his eyes and ears were still working fine. With his good arm, he tapped the button to receive the emergency call.

"—sound off. Pilots all respond." It was the Captain.

Licking the blood from his lips, Kehvan said, "P-pilot Fourteen. Active but damaged."

"Kehvan?" Seyra said before the Captain could acknowledge.

A feeling came over him at the sound of her voice. Was it relief? Crew members were grown with the knowledge that they were disposable. But knowing Seyra was still functional made him ... happy? Regulation allowed him to inquire about the well-being of fellow crewmen, so he requested, "Pilot Thirteen, condition?"

"Shaken, but not stirred," she said.

What came through the crackling speaker sounded like laughter before the Captain cut her off. "Keep channel clear. Pilot Fourteen, emergency crew assigned for extraction. Hold."

Kehvan toggled the 'message received' button instead of replying and leaned his head back to stare at the flashing screen. That was when he finally felt it. The thrumming of the propulsion engines, a sensation he'd known for all his rotations, was absent. He held up his good hand again. It felt heavier. Was this true gravity? *Last Train* had relied on the artificial stuff to prevent the crew's muscles from atrophying, and the scientists had kept it at a level they believed matched the new planet, but feeling it now, they'd been off a bit. Luckily, it was only by a little.

While he waited, Kehvan tried to get the vidscreen operational again. Finally, he managed to stop the flickering and read a partially obscured time code of *T+ 59:2**. If it was accurate, he had been unconscious for an hour. With nothing to do, he stared at the clock as it ticked up for the next thirty minutes and a handful of Pilots checked in on the emergency channel. Spread out as they were across the ship, Kehvan had only come to know the few near his sector. Aside from gathering during the Captain's speech, the last time Pilots had all been together was when the ship left Earth's orbit during the 01 generation.

The colonists.

Kehvan toggled the comm and opened a request to the bridge. When he got the signal to go ahead, he asked, "Captain?"

"Go ahead, Pilot Fourteen."

"The colonists?"

"Status unknown. Assessment ongoing. Concern logged."

"Earned some brownie points," Seyra had said to him once after he'd reported a slight temperature increase in the cryo-sleep system.

"Our duty is to maintain the well-being of the colonists and *Last Train* until the final Landing," he'd recited the crewmen's primary objective to her.

Another hour passed, then a bang sounded at the door, followed by the hissing of a plasma cutter as the extraction team made their way inside. Once it was clear, a blinding light filled the room, and Kehvan covered his eyes. The straps holding him in place were released, and he yelped when they removed the stimneedle from his broken arm. His eyes slowly adjusted to the light until he could make out two Huws and a Karal putting him on a gurney.

"Assess," he said to the Karal. Like the rest of that genetic line, the Karal was grown for medical duty. Each had the same receding hairline, dark skin, and a perpetual grimace. Solidly built and good-natured, the Huws were Basic Labor. Oddly though, one had slightly longer brown hair than the other. He would have to be checked for aberration, Kehvan noted. The Huws followed the Karal's directions as they carefully moved Kehvan out of the cockpit.

"Arm's broken. Want more? It'll have to wait," Karal shouted over the alarm. By his cadence, Kehvan knew the doctor was on downshift and had not been activated for duty before being assigned to the extraction team.

Outside the cockpit, the smoke-filled corridor was a mess. Where the white and gray paneling of the ship's interior was not completely torn apart, it was fractured beyond repair. Tube lights and ceiling tiles littered the floor, forcing the Huws to carry the gurney most of the way. Red-uniformed Crew Security continuously ran by them on their search for survivors. Even over the alarm, Kehvan could hear calls for help from side corridors.

Not until they passed a row of bodies covered by white sheets did the enormity of what had occurred finally strike him. Aside from a rare accident, unscheduled nullification was unheard of on *Last Train*. Those bodies beneath the sheets ... they were Promised Landers, just like he was. They had been destined to live out their remaining days on the new planet, with a sky above and dirt below...

"How many?" Kehvan asked, nodding at the row of corpses.

Karal shook his head sadly. "Too many."

At the medbay, the door opened only a few inches before it jammed in place, and a Huw had to pull at it to make space for the gurney. Unfortunately, the medical facility had not fared better than the rest of the ship. Contents from multiple cabinets lay spilled on the ground, and various delicate-appearing pieces of medical equipment had fallen over. Kehvan was not trained for those machines, but it was easy to tell they were broken. Karal sighed and cleared a table for the Huws to put his patient on before rummaging around on the floor.

Three bright lights in the ceiling—having somehow survived the crash—shone down on Kehvan as the longer-haired Huw pressed a button at the edge of the table. The upper part of the surface lifted beneath Kehvan's torso, sitting him up at a comfortable angle. Another button extended part of the table to his left, and Karal returned with a hand scanner which he ran over Kehvan's body. When the doctor finished, he nodded to one of the Huws, and the crewman took Kehvan's broken arm and carefully placed it on the table's extension.

"I was right. Your arm is broken. You've also got three bruised ribs and a mild concussion. Given the circumstances, I'd say you're lucky," Karal said, then took an injector from his pocket and put it to Kehvan's shoulder. The vial emptied its contents before he could even ask what it was.

The pain in his arm faded instantly, and a sense of euphoria spread like a wall of fuzziness to separate him from his body. Through that wall, Kehvan watched

Karal cut off the sleeve of his gray Pilot's jacket and poke a few times at the arm before he took it in both hands and pulled. Seeing his arm stretch and twist so unnaturally was hilarious. Somewhere in his mind, it registered as painful, but the drug-induced bliss kept that feeling from taking over.

Karal had just finished the nano-weave mesh cast on the arm when a knock came at the medbay door. The doctor nodded to one of the Huws; moments later, a blonde woman with wide green eyes appeared at Kehvan's side. She looked worried, though Kehvan couldn't figure out why. Disjointed and muffled, sounds tried to make their way into his ears, but as tired as he was, he gave up on trying to make sense of them and chose to close his eyes instead.

The pain was waiting for him when he awoke. It was less intense than the last time he had crawled out of the void, but enough to regret returning. His vision was spotty, and he rubbed at his eyes until they cleared. He was no longer the only patient in the medbay. White-uniformed

Karals attended to injured crewmembers occupying every available surface.

"Think fast," someone said, and Kehvan watched a small metal bowl fly toward his face. Instinctively, he caught it with his left hand. "Looks like you're going to be all right," Seyra said. She took the bowl from him and smiled. Her hair, usually tied back in a ponytail, hung loose against the top of her shoulders. A bit of dried blood stained her gray uniform near the right side of her neck, but Kehvan could not see any apparent injuries.

Frowning, he pointed at her hair. "Against regulation, Pilot Thirteen."

Seyra rolled her eyes. "Fuck regulation, Kehvan. Oh, *sorry*. I mean Pilot Fourteen." She motioned to all the activity around them. "It's all gone to shit, or haven't you noticed?"

Kehvan tested his left arm, but aside from some minimal pain, the mesh cast did its job. "Situation assessment," he said.

"You're lucky to be alive. How's that for an assessment? Half the ship broke off in the crash. I told the Captain we should have pulled up," she said. Kehvan registered the anger in her voice.

"Negative," Kehvan said. "Gravitation —"

Seyra yelled, "Enough!" and slammed the table right by his head, causing black spots to swim in his vision again. Then, covering her mouth, she said, "Oh! Oh no. I'm sorry, the Karal said you have a concussion." She cupped his cheek in her hand, and Kehvan could feel her fingers moving ever so slightly against his skin. It was a strange and unexpected sensation.

The same Karal from before came over, and Seyra quickly stepped back while he ran the scanner over him once more. With a grunt, he said, "No additional damage. You are on downshift for the next twenty-four hours. Doctor's orders." Looking over his shoulder at the work awaiting him, he muttered, "Lucky you."

Like the flip of a switch, Kehvan's muscles relaxed as duty regulation was lifted. "Thanks, Karal," he said.

The Medical crewman nodded and went to check on another patient.

"There's my bunkmate," Seyra said, smiling again.

Sighing, Kehvan said, "You have to stop, Seyra. Your behavior is bordering on aberration."

"Yeah, yeah," she muttered as she helped him down from the table. He was barely off it before a Huw laid another crewman in his place. Other blue-uniformed Laborers were moving equipment around at the orders of the Karals trying to organize the mess. Feeling like they were in the way now, Kehvan made for the door.

"How much of the ship is left?" he asked once they had left the medbay.

"I told you before. Just about half. Lucky for us, we were angled away from the surface."

Kehvan stopped and turned to her. "How did you bypass the Captain's order?"

"I..." she began, then paused, biting her lip. "I did what I thought was best to protect the ship."

Regulation stated that a Captain's orders could be ignored if they put the ship in danger. Satisfied with that answer, Kehvan continued down the hallway. "I'm having trouble remembering which Pilots survived. Do you have that information?"

Seyra hurried to catch up. "You can just say you're worried about them."

"Seyra, please."

Frowning, she said, "Raj, Mayla, and Estevan are all accounted for."

Kehvan felt relieved. "How long was I out this time?" Since entering the medbay, the hallway had been cleared to accommodate the increased traffic, and the alarms muted.

"A couple of hours."

He nodded.

The two walked through the ship for a few minutes in silence, then Seyra said, "Ask the question already. I know you want to."

Kehvan frowned. "The colonists?"

"The crash put a dent in the cryo-hold."

His heart skipped a beat, and he felt cold. "You mean?"

With a crooked smile, she said. "I mean, just a dent. The hull around the Earthlings is so thick I bet we could crash the ship three more times before we crack that egg." *Earthling* was a nickname the downshifted had for their cargo. It was sort of a joke. Since the crew had been created off-planet, technically, that made them aliens.

"Should have made the whole ship that tough," Kehvan said. But, even with all the deaths, he was happy to know the colonists had survived. They were the priority, after all.

Seyra laughed and slapped him on the back. Pain shot through his ribs, and he moaned while clutching his side. She quickly buried him under an avalanche of apologies.

If he was on downshift, Kehvan wanted to spend most of it in his bunk. Lucky for him, the sector that housed their crew quarters was relatively intact. He took several steps down the next corridor and noticed Seyra was no longer with him. Turning back, he saw her where the hallways diverged, standing completely still and staring at something he could not see. Returning to her side, he asked, "What is it?"

Her hand shook as she pointed to a strange red glow further down the hallway that he had somehow missed. It was unlike any light aboard *Last Train*. It had a warmth to it, almost as if it were alive. Then it dawned on him—he was seeing daylight for the first time. Somewhere down there, the hull had breached, and light from the planet's sun had found its way inside.

How could he not have seen it when she had? It was so bright, and he had been looking right at that spot before turning toward their quarters. His body stiffened when he looked directly at the alien radiance. Even now, while he was on downshift, regulation had taken control.

He felt her hand slip into his, and with a squeeze, she tugged ever so slightly as she tried to coax him to follow her into the light.

But regulation kept him in place.

In a barely audible whisper, he said, "We can't. Not yet."

Spinning to face him, she let go of his hand and said, "Why not?"

"You know why." His jaw tightened, and he took a step back.

Seyra growled, "Why can't it be us? Why do we have to wait for a popsicle's permission first?"

Popsicle? Kehvan accessed the Translink Network to make sense of the word. *A piece of flavored ice or ice cream on a stick.* Flavored ice? Oh, the colonists. "Because regulation states it has to be them."

He had backed up to the intersection leading to the quarters, but Seyra remained where she stood. She laughed bitterly as she eyed his retreat. "What's this iteration called again? The Promised Landers? Do you think we'll even get a thank you after they've woken up?"

Unsettled, Kehvan took another step back. "I... Seyra, what are you doing? Why are you talking like this?"

"Why do we even have to wake them up at all?" She spoke louder now, and nearby crew members stopped to listen. "After all, what do we really owe them? *We* died getting *them* here. Don't we deserve more than what they'll let us have?"

"I don't understand," Kehvan said, shaking his head. "None of the previous Pilot Thirteens ever spoke this way." He'd run a full replay of previous generations, all thirty iterations of her genetic line, and found no trace of this behavior.

"So? Why do I have to be like them? Why can't I be different?" She looked to the gathered onlookers in the hall. "We *can* be more. More than just... some recycled memories," she spat.

Kehvan, stunned by her words, watched as she walked away from him and toward the splash of sunlight. He didn't lift a finger or call out to her as Security emerged from another hallway to block her. She tried shoving past them, but there were just too many. Kehvan wanted to stay. To see if she would be all right. But his feet were already moving him to the quarters. His last glimpse of her was her body falling limp after a Karal came up behind her and injected something into her neck.

Maybe he had missed something, he thought hours later while staring up at the bunk above his. He ran a more detailed analysis of the Pilot Thirteen line but found no aberrations. For the most part, each had followed the established regulation of the Generational Caretaker Program of *Last Train*. Something must have happened during the crash. Her chip must be damaged; it was the only logical explanation. Though, hadn't she been acting strangely before the landing attempt? What had happened to her?

He replayed the last words she'd spoken over and over in his mind.

We can *be more. More than just… some recycled memories.*

Was that what he was? He was Pilot Fourteen, the same as all the previous Fourteens. Up until they began preparations to land, each day of the last one thousand years had followed the same pattern. What more was he supposed to be? Then, for some reason, the memory of his decantation came to him. He recalled confusion. Confusion about not knowing where, or even who, he was. Then the

Translink had activated, and all the training and memories of the previous generations flooded in. And he had understood his purpose.

"Pilot Fourteen. Follow."

Lost in thought as he was, Kehvan hadn't heard Security approach. Quickly, he sat up and placed his feet on the floor. "What is this about? I'm on downshift. I have a Karal's clearance." He showed the cast on his arm.

"Captain's orders supersede previous clearance. Comply."

The switch in his head clicked back on, and Kehvan stood rigidly. "Complying."

In silence, Security escorted him to a lift and pressed the button for the control bridge. The elevator ascended a hundred decks to the very top of *Last Train*. Kehvan-30 had never visited the bridge, but his previous iterations had, so he knew what was waiting for him as the doors slid open. From the paneled floor, his eyes drifted up to the screens that encircled the room, showing the outside of the ship.

As he stepped off the lift, he was confronted with the strange beauty of the planet's surface. Feathery plants grew in a field leading up to a chain of rust-colored mountains capped with white snow. The cameras also showed the wreckage of *Last Train* and its exposed egg-shaped cryo-hold.

"You are on downshift, yes?" said the Captain with no introduction from a raised chair at the center of the circling rows of consoles. None of the support crew looked up from their work as she spun around to face him with a stern look. Through all her wrinkles and gray hair, Kehvan could not help but see Seyra —*his* Seyra—sitting there.

Clicking his heels together, he stood at attention and said, "Previously ordered. Regulation supersedes."

With a dismissive wave, she said, "Revert to downshift."

Kehvan blinked, and his muscles relaxed.

"Better," she said. "Now, Kehvan, tell me about the earlier... incident with Pilot Thirteen."

Creases formed on his forehead as his brow knitted in confusion. It was unlike the Captain to speak with such familiarity. "I don't understand, sir."

Fingers tapping rhythmically on one armrest, she crossed her legs. "I want you to tell me what might have caused the Seyra's aberrant behavior."

"Is there an issue with the Translink upload, sir?" A function of the chip in their heads was to store and archive every experience for the next generation.

Her lips pursed for a second, then she said, "I want to hear *your* perspective."

This is odd, he thought and glanced at the support crew to see if any of them had noticed, but none gave any sign. Then, looking back at her, he saw she was growing impatient. Kehvan did not know how to begin. He had never needed to describe something before.

"Come on, out with it," Seyra-29 said, waving a hand to hurry him up.

Kehvan swallowed as he collected his thoughts, then told her everything that happened up to Seyra's outburst. After he had finished, he asked, "Could it be a reaction to something in the planet's atmosphere? Are the air circulators malfunctioning?"

Ignoring his questions, the Captain pressed her palms together. Resting her chin on her fingertips, and, with her gaze burrowing into him, she asked, "What exactly did she say to you?"

Her scrutiny made him uncomfortable. Was there an issue with the Translink Hub? Had it been damaged during the crash? Was that why she couldn't access either his or Seyra's uploads? Kehvan pinged the central network and found it functioning correctly.

"It was recorded, sir. I can find an Engineer if you need help… to…" his voice trailed off because several of the green-uniformed Engineers were already on the bridge.

Eyes narrowing, the Captain asked, "What are you hiding, Kehvan?"

"Hiding, sir?"

Sitting back in her chair, the Captain clasped her hands in her lap. "Kehvans are dutiful and dedicated," she said. "Always have been. Kehvan-29 was a good friend of mine, just as you are to Seyra-30." The Captain paused a moment before continuing. "It's difficult when a previous generation overlaps the next. There are… feelings you want to express, but that would go against regulation and serve no purpose. I don't envy you, Kehvan, not with two Seyras in your life." A sad smile flashed briefly before vanishing. "We're a willful genetic line."

Then her face grew serious once more. "But we've always done what is required of us. That is, until now. This is why I want you to help me understand."

How could she expect him to explain something he didn't understand? Should he tell her about his own abnormal thoughts since Seyra's incident? Were they sick? Was there a virus in the Translink System? Could it spread to others?

The Captain sighed, letting her shoulders sag. "You truly don't know, do you?"

The corner of Kehvan's eye twitched. He felt utterly useless. "I... Captain..."

The chair's compad chimed before he could continue. Frowning, she glanced at the display, and under her breath, she muttered, "What now?" In response, words scrolled on the small screen until she finally toggled it off and looked back at him. "Say you were in my position, Kehvan. What would you do with her?"

Sweat trickled down his back—none of this made sense. The questions, the abnormal behaviors, the landing, it was all getting to be too much. Maybe the concussion was affecting him more than he realized.

The Captain sighed again. "Pilot Fourteen, comply with inquiry."

Even as the storm raged inside his mind, Kehvan reverted. "Per regulation, aberrant crewmembers must be nullified. Begin decantation of generation thirty-one of Pilot Thirteen. Recommend quarantine of current generation's memories until factor causing behavior identified and revert to generation twenty-nine Translink download."

The Captain nodded while combing her fingers through her hair. "Kehvans were the best Captains. They always ran a tight ship."

From the archives, Kehvan recalled that his previous iterations had found the position quite lonely. Each generation's lifespan was dictated by which category of crew you were in. For Pilots, it was thirty-five years. So, even though the new generation looked, sounded, and acted the same as the previous one, they were not *truly* the ones you had served with for years.

"Revert to downshift," the Captain ordered.

When he did, she asked, "Do you really think I should nullify Seyra? Is that what you want?"

No. I'd promised to see the sky with her. Without hesitation, he said, "For the sake of the colonists, it would be for the best."

The Captain closed her eyes and leaned on the armrest. "Concern logged," she said as she cradled the side of her head in her hand.

Since the launch of *Last Train*, the ship could have been run solely on their optimism alone, but now it just felt... different. Almost as if their morale had been stripped away in the crash. He knew the dead would be retrieved, recycled, and their protein used to build the next generations, just as the program had been designed. The crew would continue. It had to. Work still needed to be done before the colonists could be revived. Their purpose hadn't changed, so what had?

The Captain's compad sounded again, but she did not bother to answer. Instead, she nodded to the Security. "Take him to Seyra. Maybe her behavior will correct if she talks to this Kehvan."

This Kehvan.

As he rode the lift down from the bridge, those words bounced around inside his skull. Something about them bothered him; he only hoped it wasn't a precursor to aberration.

By design, *Last Train* had no crime; the regulatory control of the Translink System prevented such things. Therefore, it had no need for a brig. Security was the least utilized and least important in the ship's hierarchy, but they could command crewmembers in emergencies. All of this meant that, without a proper place to keep her, Seyra was confined to a storage room on the thirty-second deck.

The Security crewman led with a purposeful gait, while Kehvan tentatively followed and often had to hurry to keep up. He had never been so lost within his own mind. He began to question his actions, searching for abnormalities that might have formed since the crash. There was a sinking feeling in his gut that he had never felt before. Why was he suddenly nervous about seeing Seyra? He had to admit that he was afraid. Afraid that she was not the same person he remembered.

Except for the occasional working light, the deck was dark. He had to be careful not to crack his head against anything knocked loose. At the end of one corridor, a second Security crewman stood at a closed door. The red-coated crewman stepped aside when they arrived, and after a slight hesitation, Kehvan pressed the button beside the door.

The squeal of the hatch reverberated loudly in the otherwise quiet hallway. The room within wasn't spacious. It had been packed full at the beginning of *Last Train*'s journey, but only a few secured plastic crates were left after all these centuries.

Seyra was on the floor opposite the entryway, her back against the wall, legs pulled up to her chest, and face buried in her hands. She'd removed her jacket and thrown it in the corner, where it lay wrinkled and discarded. Stepping inside, Kehvan hoped she'd be asleep, as it would make an excellent excuse to leave. The door screeched closed behind him, sealing the two inside, alone. No, not alone. Cameras monitored every inch of the ship, so someone would be observing them. That thought did not ease his newly acquired fears.

Fears of what?

The reality was that he simply wanted her to be the old Seyra. The one that had loved to joke with him and tried to make him laugh. Because if she was not, if she was the one that had attempted to make him leave the ship, then she would have to be nullified.

"Seyra?" he asked and felt the dryness in his mouth. Working his tongue around, he built up some saliva and tried again. "Seyra? Are you awake?"

Slowly, she shifted and let out a long breath. Then, brushing her hair back, she raised her head and met his stare with bloodshot eyes. "You can come closer. I'm not some wild animal."

Earlier, she had acted like one when she fought to get past Security. He'd never seen someone behave that way, and he had to admit it was disturbing. But this was Seyra. His bunkmate. His friend. Kehvans and Seyras had always been friends. Trying to hide his trepidation, Kehvan stood straight and went to stand at her feet.

She didn't look up to meet his eyes this time, so Kehvan crouched down. Forcing a smile, he asked, "Better?"

"I suppose it'll have to do." She put on an equally fake grin, but it faded as she asked, "What are you doing here?"

"The Captain wanted me to come and see you."

She looked at him sideways with her cheek resting on one knee. "Why?"

"Honestly, I don't know. Her questions didn't make sense to me."

"What questions?"

"Well," he rocked back on his heels until he was sitting on the floor, "she wanted to know what happened leading up to the, uh, incident."

"What did you say?" she asked, cocking an eyebrow.

He found he couldn't look away from the intensity in her eyes. And he didn't want to. "I told her what happened. But I don't know why she needed me to do that in the first place."

A sad but triumphant smile formed on her lips as she said, "Probably because she was missing my upload."

Kehvan smiled. "Missing your upload? So, your Translink *is* damaged?" Here it was, the answer he had needed to hear. He'd report it, they'd fix her chip, and everything would be back to normal. He felt relieved. But that was only short-lived.

She shook her head. "No. It isn't damaged. I removed it."

Kehvan lost the ability to speak as he stared at her, frozen and eyes bulging.

Seyra closed hers and, still smiling, said, "I'll go ahead and answer the next question for you. Haven't you ever wanted something that was yours alone?" Tucking her legs in beneath her, she slid down until she lay on her side and rested her head on her hands like a pillow. "That's why."

Kehvan stared at her for a long time after she stopped speaking, with her eyes closed. He was afraid she had fallen asleep, but then she shifted, and looked up at him. Fighting his own mouth, he managed to finally ask, "How?"

"It wasn't hard. Just a slice behind the ear, some tweezers, a mirror, and string. She rolled onto her back and tilted her head toward the wall. Brushing the hair aside, she revealed a sutured scar the length of his thumb behind her right ear. It was red and swollen and looked painful.

"Why?" was the next word he was able to say.

"Out of all the generations since the first, we're distinct. We're the Promised Landers. And I... I wanted to keep that for myself. I didn't want to pass it on to the future Seyra," she said. Then, a sound that could have been either a laugh or a sob escaped her lips, and her hand covered her mouth as she blinked back tears.

"That... was selfish," Kehvan said. He wanted to take her hand, to comfort her, but he didn't.

Seyra shook her head and clutched the collar of her shirt as she said, "And then, when I took it out, I found something, Kehvan."

"Found? Found what?"

Tears flowing freely now, she whispered, "Me," and her chest heaved as she wept. There was no sadness in her glistening eyes, only a mysterious happiness just beneath the surface.

An unexpected tightness gripped Kehvan's heart at seeing her cry. Softly, he said, "Explain."

"Are you sure?" she whispered back, staring up, not at him, but at the ceiling.

Though the monitors would clearly hear them, and perhaps that was what Seyra wanted anyway, he said, "Tell me."

"A strange thought came to me before the Captain's speech. What was going to happen after we landed?" she said.

Kehvan knew the answer to that. "We wake up the primary colonists."

"No. After that."

Kehvan accessed the landing itinerary. "Primary colonists establish the initial settlement. Crew Labor, Engineering, Medical, and Security report directly to them. Once colony deemed habitable, next wave of colonists revived."

Seyra nodded, a sneer twisting her mouth into something ugly. "Just like regulation states."

"Because that's how it is going to happen," Kehvan said.

Anger edged into her voice. "You've never thought about what's missing in the itinerary, have you?"

What could be missing? The itinerary had been devised well before the construction of *Last Train*. "Then we'll see the sky?"

"Will we?"

"I don't know what you mean," he said.

"Where do the Pilots fit in the itinerary?"

The question hit him harder than the console had during the crash. Sounds escaped his lips, but none of them were words.

"I'll make it easy for you. We don't. Once we landed, our purpose was complete. We're obsolete now, Kehvan." She turned to look at him and reached over to take his hand. He let her, and it felt... good.

He asked, "Is that why you don't want to wake the colonists?"

Abruptly she let his hand go and rolled over to face the wall. "You can't stop, can you?"

Rubbing his fingers together, he tried to hold on to the sensation of her skin against his. "Stop what?"

"Being what you were created to be."

"I have to. It's our purpose," he said. What other way was there?

She looked over her shoulder, but not at him, and said, "I want you to be different. No, I *need* you to be. For me, Kehvan... Please."

"Different from what?"

"From all the other Kehvans," she said and rolled away from the wall. Looking hesitant, she clenched her jaw at first, then, with trembling lips, she whispered, "Because you're *my* Kehvan. And I want to be *your* Seyra."

He smiled again, reassuring her, "Each of our iterations have been friends. That's how it's always been."

Once more, she turned away from him, and no matter how many questions he asked, Seyra refused to answer.

After returning to his quarters, Kehvan studied his reflection in the mirror. Lifting the brown hair from his forehead, he looked at the deep purple bruise he'd acquired from the crash. He carefully touched it, then let the hair fall back into place. His bottom lip had been split open, and an ugly scab tugged at the rosy flesh whenever he moved his mouth. Finally, he stared into his hazel eyes. They were the same eyes every Kehvan had seen in the same mirror for the last thousand years.

I want you to be different.

I don't know what that means. Nothing had made sense after the crash. It had to be the concussion. *How can I be different? Isn't this who I'm supposed to be?* The unblinking eyes appeared lost, set adrift without a purpose. Maybe it was the extended downshift. Once he got back to duty and continued training...

Training for what? What else is there for us to do? There had to be something. One of the other Pilots must know. Looking away from the mirror, he tapped his compad and requested all remaining Pilots to check in. Of the seventeen, only eight had survived the crash. He dialed in on Raj and linked with his pad, and Pilot Seventeen filled the tiny screen. Raj, an exhausted-looking brown-skinned man with messy black hair, had a bandage on his cheek.

"Nice of you to finally call," Raj said.

"Oh, I believe I made a mistake. I was trying to reach Estevan," Kehvan said with a half-hearted laugh.

Raj gave him a tired chuckle. "You'll just have to settle for me. What's the inquiry?"

Kehvan muted the pad for a moment and looked to see if any of the crew in the quarters were paying attention to the conversation. With the number of injured and dead from the crash, the quarters were only at minimum capacity. Satisfied they weren't listening, he turned and placed his pad on the shelf below the mirror and unmuted.

"What's your status?"

Raj let out a yawn and scratched the back of his head. "My status? I'm downshifted. You?"

"Same." He showed Raj his cast. "Everyone else?"

"All downshifted. Not much use for us now that we've landed," Raj said. "Don't mind it, really. We get to sit around while the others do the rest of the work."

"How long is your downshift?"

Raj said, "When given? Twenty-four hours."

"Same for me."

Raj nodded. "Same for all Pilots."

Kehvan thought for a moment, then asked, "Raj, what do you want to do once we're allowed off the ship?"

"Off the ship?" Raj asked. He scratched at the edge of the bandage on his cheek. "I never really thought about it. I don't know."

Kehvan felt a stirring in his stomach. "I see."

"Why? Have you?"

It wasn't a secret, but Kehvan had only shared his dream of seeing the sky with only one other person before this—Seyra. Their exchanges were all archived and available for anyone to access if they wanted to. *Last Train* had no secrets. At least, it hadn't.

Kehvan shook his head and felt like he was going to be sick. The protein paste he'd ingested earlier was making an unscheduled reappearance. He looked down at the sink and let a dribble of bile spill from his mouth. He waved his hand at the sensor and splashed cold water on his face. He heard Raj ask if something was wrong and if he was okay.

Water running off his chin, Kehvan said, "There's nothing you'd rather be than a Pilot?"

Raj tilted his head. "I don't understand the question."

"That's all, Raj. End transmission."

"Transmission ended," Raj said.

The screen went black, and Kehvan threw up.

After cleaning himself off, Kehvan lay in his bunk and tried to figure out what was wrong with him. Had Seyra done this to him? In the questions she'd ask him when they were alone, the 'private' conversations they'd had over the years that the monitors didn't flag as against regulation, had she knowingly implanted a desire in him for something beyond the landing? He wanted to find something to blame, but when he tried to put it all on Seyra, he couldn't.

It had to be his chip, a glitch he couldn't detect because of a malfunction. He'd report it to the Engineers in charge of the Translink System. Instead of using his compad, Kehvan thought it would be easier to just go down to the Hub in his sector and save a lot of time if they had to repair it. Unconsciously, he touched the small bump behind his right ear.

Hauling himself off the bunk, he felt only incrementally better as he staggered out of the quarters. He discovered that regulation had been updated as he passed the hallway with the hull breach. Per the new regulation, Kehvan quickly moved away from the corridor and headed straight for the lift, unable to even look to see if the sunlight was still present. Did he only know it was there because Seyra had shown him? Was there more he might have missed because regulation prevented him from experiencing it? "No," he said quietly. Regulation had its purpose, and so did he. Humanity needed both of them.

At the other end of the hallway, a team of Huws were repairing the damage to the lighting tubes. The sound of their pneumatic wrenches gave Kehvan a piercing headache. He'd never experienced anything like it. Something had to be wrong. Not relying on the Translink chip in case it was damaged, he pulled up the symptoms for a concussion on the compad and found he was suffering from most of them. Nothing about this felt mild, as the Karal had diagnosed. Now there was something else he'd have to report.

He made it to the lift and requested the deck for the Translink Hub, and the doors hissed shut. He leaned back against the wall, eyes closed, as he tried to will his head to stop throbbing. Focusing on the steady rhythm of the lift, the ambient noise was similar enough to the now silent engines that it managed to soothe some of the pain.

When he arrived at the Hub, he reported the glitch. An Engineer explained that there was a backlog of issues caused by the crash, and it would take time to get to them all, and he would chime Kehvan's compad when it was his turn. Kehvan thanked the Engineer and was on his way back to the lift when his pad chirped. *That was fast*, he thought, but then he saw it was a ship-wide communication from the Captain.

"Crew of *Last Train*, we've arrived on the new planet. It might not be how we'd intended to land, but here we are. In the coming days, we will begin the reviving process of the primary colonists. But before that, we will need to decant a sizable number of crew to replace the ones we've lost. Labor, Medical, and Engineering are priority. Security remains at acceptable levels."

The Captain's face looked away from her screen for a moment, and Kehvan thought he saw her brush something from her eye. When she looked back, her expression was like steel. "Surviving Pilots, await summons to Genetics."

Genetics? Only twice in their lifetime was a crewmember at Genetics—decantation and nullification. Kehvan's heart felt like it was close to bursting from his chest.

Where do the Pilots fit in the itinerary?

When the message ended, Kehvan found Raj on his compad and dialed in. The other Pilot answered, but Kehvan could already see Raj was on duty, his face expressionless. "Pilot Fourteen, inquiry?"

"Raj, where are you?" Kehvan asked, looking up and down the hallway. Huws and Engineers were close by, but none could hear him.

"In route to Genetics, per Captain's order," Raj said.

Kehvan closed the channel and ran.

He found Raj sitting in a chair, his back stiff, inside the Genetics Factory's waiting area. The room was empty, with only two other doors and one chair. One door was an exit for the newly decanted crew, and the other led to nullification. The chair was positioned in front of the latter. Kehvan had no idea what he hoped to accomplish as he barreled into the room and rushed to stand before Raj. Regulation didn't prevent him from being here, but he wouldn't be allowed to interfere with the nullification process. He wanted to shake Raj. To keep him from going through with the process, but he couldn't. Kehvan could only stand there.

A Karal studying a compad entered and almost ran into Kehvan. If the Medical crewmember was surprised, his face didn't show as he looked up from the device in his hand and said, "Pilot Fourteen. Early for scheduled arrival."

Kehvan found the words he was allowed to say on the matter, "I wanted to see Pilot Seventeen off."

The Karal nodded. "Nullification scheduled for zero four hundred. Expected completion of all Pilots in eight hours."

"Decantation of next iteration?" Kehvan said, afraid that he already knew the answer.

"Negative. Genetic purpose complete."
We're obsolete now, Kehvan.

He couldn't breathe. He needed air. Holding onto the wall for support, he managed to get out of Genetics before he dialed Mayla. Her narrow eyes, a trait inherited from the genetic source of her line, were just as blank as Raj's had been. Did they all look like that when they were on duty? How had he never noticed that before? Kehvan ended the transmission before it even began and tried Estevan.

Estevan had tan skin with dark hair, and Kehvan was relieved to see a pillow behind his head. "Wrong compad, right?" Estevan said.

Kehvan shook his head. "Estevan, listen. I think your summons is next."

Estevan nodded. "I was talking to Mayla when her order came through."

"How long ago was that?"

"A few minutes," Estevan said. The screen shifted as he rolled onto his side.

Kehvan wanted to tell Estevan to ignore the order, but he couldn't. So instead, he asked, "What did you want to do after we landed?"

Raising an eyebrow, Estevan said, "I never thought about it."

"Ending transmission," Kehvan said and turned the screen off.

Clutching his compad, Kehvan wanted to scream, to rush back into Genetics and demand Raj revert to downshift. He wanted to find a way to keep them all from being nullified. There was no hiding on this ship; cameras were everywhere. And once they gave the order, he'd line up to be nullified just like the rest. But he didn't want that. He wanted to see the sky. And more than anything, he wanted to see it with Seyra.

Seyra, he thought. After today, there would be no more Seyra. She would be gone, the same as him. No more iterations meant no more memories. It struck him then that this was what the colonists must have felt before someone came up with the plan for *Last Train*. This was the fear of missing what came next, of not seeing someone you care about ever again. This was the fear of death. He would never feel her hand in his again, never see her crack a smile. He would never see the sky with her.

That wasn't what Kehvan wanted. What he wanted was to be with her.

Not wanting to draw attention as he made his way back to the lift, Kehvan did not run. He rode it down three levels and then went inside a supply closet, where cameras spied on him even in such an unimportant part of the ship. He wanted to smash the reflective lenses, but he couldn't. His hand went to the lump behind his ear. Just beneath his skin, the wire mesh monitored for violations and would immobilize him at any sign that he was about to break regulation. There was no pain in it, but not having control of one's body was highly unsettling, and the first generation had found it easier to simply comply, as had each iteration since. Now, it felt like he was one of those puppet toys he had seen on a ripvid that could only do whatever the strings allowed.

Time was running short, he knew, so he flung the contents off shelves. All he needed was something sharp. That's what Seyra had said. It was just a little cut. At last, he picked up a bulkhead patch kit and removed a small square of metal about the size of his palm. This was not the item's intended purpose, but it would have to do.

Tilting his head to the side, Kehvan placed the corner against his skin and froze. He couldn't continue. He wanted to, but it was against regulation. Trapped in his own head, he screamed. Then the compad on his belt chimed a priority message.

A Security crewman's voice came out of the speaker, "Pilot Fourteen. Scheduled activation advanced. Report to Genetics. Com—" the remainder of the command mysteriously cut off. But another order could come at any moment.

Kehvan's thoughts raced as he struggled to violate what he had been created to uphold. There had to be a way. Seyra had done it, and she was just as wired up as him. He couldn't even move his head. How did she do it? How? His thoughts whirled until he couldn't think anymore. And that's when the answer came to him: the ripvids.

Seyra-01 had figured out that the only way to view them—and for others to watch —was to overtask their Translink chip by manually uploading the entirety of their archived memories while simultaneously running a diagnostic. The entire process only took a few seconds, but that was more than enough time to watch a memory clip.

It had to work, he thought. Letting out a breath, Kehvan connected his Translink and began the upload of a thousand years of memories. Then ran the diagnostic.

A Security crewman found him in the closet.

"Pilot Fourteen. Follow. Comply."

"Complying," Kehvan said and followed him out of the closet, where they passed by other crewmembers going about their business.

Together, they entered the lift, and the button for the Genetics deck was pressed. Kehvan was silent, his hands clasped behind his back as he stared straight ahead. Finally, the elevator stopped, Security stepped off, and Kehvan hit the button for deck thirty-two.

He had expected alarms as he exited the lift, but it was silent in the dark hallway except for the constant chirping of his compad, which he ignored. That alone felt both strange and exhilarating. He had no way of knowing if the storage room was still guarded, and he didn't care. Kehvan ripped off a broken conduit from the wall and made his way to Seyra.

It wasn't until he rounded the corner, prepared to fight his way through, and found it empty, that he chose to finally answer the compad. It was only an incoming text message from an unknown source.

>*You have ten minutes to get her off my ship.*

He stared at the message for a second, puzzled by what it meant. Get her off my ship? "Captain?" he asked.

>*Ten minutes. That's all I can give you.*

"Why are you helping me?"

>*I'm not helping you. I'm helping her.*

"How?"

>*I'm taking that answer to my nullification. I'm just glad one of us finally made it through to one of you. Now, ten minutes.*

The transmission ended.

Ten minutes. It was enough time. They weren't far from the lift that went down to their quarters. And from there, the breach. Whatever came after that, so be it. What he had to say now was more important.

Kehvan opened the door to the storage room and stepped inside. Just as he had left her, Seyra lay on the ground with her back to the entrance. The makeshift weapon slipped from his hand and clattered to the floor as he knelt by her.

Quietly, he said, "Seyra?"

She did not respond.

His hand shaking, Kehvan reached over and touched her arm. Drawing in a sharp breath, Seyra turned her head and looked up at him. He wanted to cry, so he did.

"Kehvan? What are you doing?" she asked, rolling over.

"Seyra." It was all he could say.

She rose to her knees and took hold of his shoulders. "Kehvan, what's happened? Are you damaged again?" Her hand came away with flecks of blood on her fingers.

He took her hand and held it tightly. "You've always been," he said when he could find the words.

"Been what?" Her eyes looked so worried, so beautiful.

"*My* Seyra."

See Dan Le Fever's story "Trapped in Memory"
online at Metaphorosis.
If you liked it, leave a comment. Authors love
that!
Remember to subscribe to our e-mail updates so
you'll know when new stories are posted.

About the story

"Trapped in Memory" comes from my desire to write something new. Previously, I had focused on horror, Gothic, and post-apocalyptic genres, and I had always been a fan of sci-fi, so I thought, why not give it a shot? Whenever I'm writing, I listen to music. I try to pick a band or musical style that fits what emotions I'm trying to convey, and this time I chose a Norwegian folk group called Wardruna. Their songs give me a feeling of loneliness, sadness, and anger, but also hope. These emotions are what I hope the reader gets as they read my story. Over the last two years, I think the majority of us are on the same wavelength with the isolation and human detachment we've experienced because of the pandemic, and I felt it was an excellent theme to explore. I saw myself in Kehvan's shoes, trying to make sense of what I was experiencing but wanting to find a way to break out of the bubble I'd been placed in. Luckily, I have my wife to keep me sane, but it had been a difficult two years. And in the end, it is a story of change. The patterns we follow in life are comforting, but is that all we can hope for, or is there more out there for us?

A question for the author

Q: What book or books inspired you as a child?

A: Frank Herbert's *Dune* is one of my biggest influences. I would not be the person today if it had not been for that book. Next, would be all three *Dragonlance Chronicles* by Margaret Weis and Tracy

Hickman. And as I got a little older, *Fight Club* by Chuck Palahniuk.

About the author

Dan Le Fever is just a guy from Lynn, MA with a degree in history from Salem State College, with a focus on Byzantine and Ottoman history. He is also fascinated by linguistics, etymology, and orthography. When he isn't writing, Dan spends his time playing video games, watching horror/sci-fi entertainment, and practicing American Kenpo.

danlefever.wordpress.com, @lefeverdan

Heart Moon

R. Gatwood

The old pop song says it's in his kiss, but of course that's nonsense. The only way to know if your man's love is true is to cut out his heart and eat it, still beating, by the light of the full moon.

You'll dither over the decision, of course. You'll collect the ingredients and sharpen the dagger, only to abandon the project halfway. A few months later you'll start again. For him, a simple infusion of opium and valerian and chamomile, to drug him to sleep. For you, a mix of lemon and mugwort and green tea and a smidgen of psilocybin, for alertness and perception of liminal things. It'll be the biggest spell you've ever done. The one that makes you a real witch and not just a bullshit herbalist who knows a few parlor tricks. (Let's just say the ritual consumption of a human heart is a serious power boost.) You won't have to feel inferior to your witch friends anymore.

Scheduling your camping trip for the full moon shouldn't be hard, but it is. At the last minute his buddy will invite him to a beer tasting in town, and the two of you will argue irritably over whether to change plans. (If he loved you, would he give in? Or is that a ridiculous question?) Finally (maybe because you love him—or think you do), you will agree to go to the tasting and leave for the campsite right afterwards. It'll be more fun than you expected. You're not much of a beer lover, but they will have an amazing grapefruit shandy that you buy a six-pack of, and watching Dave lick IPA off the stubble above his lip will make something flutter inside you. For the hundredth time, you will reconsider whether to kill him. But you've already got the battery-powered bone saw and ritual dagger and folding shovel stashed away in your camping pack. And you've already agonized over this long enough. He will let out a burp and grin. The moment will pass.

On the way back to the car his hand will be a soft knobby animal in yours. "That was good," he'll say.

"Yeah," you will admit.

He will stop, tug you close, and kiss the top of your head. Beer and mustard on his breath. "Thanks for, you know, compromising. Don't worry. I'll get us there safe." He'll have promised to drive the whole way to the campsite.

"I know." You'll mean it.

Sometimes you think you hate him.

He says "I love you" like it's easy. Maybe too easy. Your friends tell you he's the perfect guy. Maybe too perfect, is what you'll think as you sit beside him in his comfortable old Prius, listening to him hum along to the playlist you made him. There's got to be something wrong with him. Why else would he be with you? Mentally, you'll list off your flaws: constantly seeking reassurance; obsessed with your witch career; depressingly mediocre at most things, including witchcraft; tentatively murderous. Also just generally perverse. When your best friend got her breast cancer diagnosis, you were frantic—but when it turned out to be terminal, you felt relieved. You prefer certainty to hope.

Dave grew up with parents who loved and supported him, you're pretty sure. You grew up with well-meaning but self-absorbed types who hugged you tenderly one day and forgot your tae kwon do match the next. Now your mom is too wrapped up in her Valium and her church gossip to think much about you or your siblings, and your dad has gotten gruff and politically off-putting the way older men sometimes do. The birthday cards they send you are as generic as something you'd get for a casual acquaintance. You don't waste time on family these days.

In place of family you have your witch friends—most of them more advanced than you—and Dave. You watch his face a lot, preferably when he won't notice you're looking. When you ask what he's thinking about, he says, "I dunno. Work stuff. You. Uh, what we're gonna have for dinner." Maddening. There has to be more. If you pry—if you dig up his exes, his unspoken ambitions, his childhood traumas (?), his taboo fantasies (??), his doubts about your relationship (???)—will he leave? You know he at least thinks he loves you; he's too decent a guy to lead you on. But people don't always know their own emotions.

Case in point: You're not absolutely sure you love him. You're obsessed, certainly. You have secret Excel spreadsheets detailing his likes and dislikes. Squeezing his biceps, scenting his arousal gives you a shot of adrenaline and desire. You've inadvertently memorized the threads of gold in his eyes. You're also planning to kill him.

You once read a book about Sada Abe, a woman who famously strangled her lover in the 1930s and kept his penis as a precious souvenir. "I loved him so much," she said, "I wanted him all to myself." Abe was on to something. If she'd been a witch, she would have appreciated the power of quite a different organ.

A real witch, the kind of witch you're studying to be, knows there's no such thing as a love spell. You can't make someone love you, can't really keep them all to yourself. But you can gain knowledge of another person's soul, at the cost of destroying them. Which is worth it, isn't it? To sacrifice your relationship on the altar of certainty? To gain power, too, beyond what you've ever dared to hope for?

Isn't it?

By the time you arrive at the campsite, you'll have only an hour and a half before the moon is directly above. He'll think you're adorably eager, rushing to lug your packs out of the back the second he's parked. When you tell him you want to camp in the clearing near the creek, he'll say sure. The clearing will be open to the sky and the creek will help you wash off the evidence.

Calculating the trajectory of the moon, you'll hang your pot over the fire, and you'll make your two cups of tea. One for him, one for you. You'll ask him to try the new blend you created, and he'll perk up. He loves being your taste tester.

"Hmmmmm," he will say after his first sip. You'll hold your breath, wondering if you pulled off your attempt at a smooth earthy flavor. It doesn't matter, you'll tell yourself, as long as he drinks the whole thing (he always does), but you'll resent how badly you want his opinion. He'll say,

"Sultry, strident, with a playful impertinence."

You will throw a twig at him.

"It's delicious, Amy, seriously. Little strong, but good. Some chamomile in there?"

"Yeah. Good eye."

"More like good tongue," he'll say, the innuendo casual, incidental.

You'll smile at each other, enjoying a shared private knowledge. You're almost certain he doesn't tell his buddies about your sex life. Which doesn't prove anything, of course.

"What are you calling it?" He likes the names you make up for your potions.

You'll ponder a moment. "Heart Moon."

He will nod. "Perfect," he'll say softly, and he'll take another sip, his hazel eyes golden in the firelight.

Soon those eyes will start to droop, and when you tease him, he'll mumble with faux grumpiness about not being sleepy. He'll invite you into the sleeping bag as he plumps the pillow, and you'll say, "Later, I want to sit by the fire a while." It might be the last time you see him awake. His eyes will fall shut too fast.

What you're looking for isn't to be found in his eyes, however, any more than in his kiss.

It won't take him long to slip into a deep, deep slumber. Deep enough that when you roll him onto his back (he's a side sleeper, always seeming to reach out to you across the mattress), he won't so much as twitch. You've watched him sleep many times. As ever, he'll be handsome in his sleep. You'll hate it. You're certain you've never looked that good in your sleep, and you suspect if you asked him, he'd lie to spare your feelings.

You'll open the sleeping bag with damp, shaky fingers. The zipper will sound louder than it should despite the murmur of crickets, the rumble of the distant road, the hoot of an owl. The moon, six minutes away from being exactly overhead, will feel like a spotlight. You'll strip efficiently despite your trembling, leaving your clothes on the other side of the fire.

You'll draw the dagger and anoint it with the daisy oil just like you practiced, then lay it beside you. You'll grip the bone saw. Your own heart will pound as you straddle his hips, jostling him just enough to tip his head to the side. You'll push up his thin T-shirt. Beneath it his skin will be scattered with pale hairs that vanish briefly as a cloud passes overhead. His breastbone will thump with a strong, slow beat.

Your eyes and fingers will trace along the bottom of his rib cage, then, for no real reason, back up to where the T-shirt is bunched under his armpits. There you'll find a hard lump in his shirt pocket and, curious despite or because of your nerves, you'll pull it out. A square box flocked with velvet.

You'll stare at it, run a thumb over the seam of the lid, and find yourself shaking with rage. You'll be holding the bone saw in your dominant right hand, so it's with your left that you'll hurl the box ineffectually into the grass. Of course. Of course he had plans of his own this whole time. It will feel like a sick joke. Something deliberately placed in your path to derail you. This whole time you've been brewing your selfish, pathetic, needy scheme, he's been dreaming of white picket fences and His-and-Hers towels. No, you'll think, that's not fair. His imagination isn't quite that bourgeois. He's been dreaming of—what?

Still quivering, clutching the bone saw close to you, you'll think for the thousandth time about how you've never quite figured out what's going on inside him. That's the question that haunts you every time he smiles, every time he says love. The question you're so close to getting an answer to. You'll stare at his peaceful profile.

The sound of your phone will make you jump. The alarm will be set to play a carefully chosen song. It'll be timed so that when the singer hits the high note in the third verse, the moon will be directly overhead to the minute, and your dagger will sever his—

And then you'll do it, of course. You'll have come all this way, prepared so carefully. The saw will buzz powerfully as you run it up his sternum, spattering warm wetness over your naked body. You'll toss the saw to the side and pry his rib cage open. You'll raise the dagger and slice through the vessels that surround the squirming fist of muscle. And at last, muttering the words of the spell, you'll seize the oracular organ in your bare hands and bring it to your teeth.

You'll know.

You'll know he loves you. Loved you. The ring box in his breast pocket, yeah, it's a cliché, white veils and tossed bouquets, but it was real. It was sincere. All those times you tried to decipher his silences and thoughtful gestures, he was loving you. The knowledge will flood your bloody mouth, almost too much to swallow.

Or: You'll know he didn't love you. Bitter knowledge, but as satisfying as canines tearing through raw flesh. All those times he whispered to you in the sweaty dark, brought you chocolates along with the tampons you asked him to pick up, shopped hopefully for a ring, he was just being his good-natured self. He may have thought he loved you. He never wanted to hurt you—of that you'll be sure. Like so many people, he's spent his life blinkered and clueless, chasing what he thinks will make him happy, and why shouldn't it make him happy to marry a witch?

Or: You won't do it after all. You'll never find out what you want to know, never be as great a witch as you could be. You're such a cliché, you'll think, sniveling, unbloodied but bowed over his dozing form. One little token of affection and you cave to the conventional life. Do you even want to get married? Maybe it wasn't the ring that changed your mind, you'll think as the song from your phone reaches the high note and plays on. Maybe it was just him. Maybe it was just you.

So those are the possibilities. You'll have a choice to make, or not just one choice but many along the way. You may have a grave to dig. You may have a ring box to search for in the tall grass, waving your phone's flashlight around and cursing under your breath. You may have a man, a good man, an oblivious man, to roll back onto his side in the down sleeping bag. You may have a lonely hike back to the car in the dim light of dawn. You may have regrets: a full moon wasted, or a lover dead.

Now choose.

See R. Gatwood's story "Heart Moon" online at Metaphorosis.
If you liked it, leave a comment. Authors love that!
Remember to subscribe to our e-mail updates so you'll know when new stories are posted.

About the story

Honestly, the main inspiration for this story was "The Shoop Shoop Song (It's in His Kiss)". I was only vaguely familiar with it, possibly from Cher's cover, when I heard my friends singing it. I pointed out that, if his face was just his charms and his embrace was just his arms, then his kiss must be just his lips. They asked how, then, could you know if he loves you so? My answer was the second sentence of "Heart Moon".

Of course, an interesting premise is nothing without execution. I struggled through several drafts to show how the main character half loves, half hates her wonderful boyfriend; wants to have him all to herself, wants to kill him; and craves to know whether he loves her, maybe even at the cost of his life. My thanks to my lovely writing workshop and to B. Morris Allen at *Metaphorosis*, who helped.

A question for the author

Q: What's an idea you're dying to write but haven't, and why?

A: I've long wanted to write a cyberpunk story about racial injustice, but my efforts have dissatisfied me. In the story, a bug in neuro implant software would leave people losing touch with the physical world and behaving like sleepwalkers, leading them to be mistaken for zombies by panicky gun owners and police officers. Sometimes the writer who has the idea isn't the right person to write it. Perhaps someone else will.

About the author

R. Gatwood is the emergent consciousness of a spectacularly inefficient library shelving system. It writes short fiction and occasionally text games, and it also enjoys tea, bourbon, podcasts, and trees. (Best not to ask how a shelving system can enjoy those things.)

iwantanewhead.wordpress.com, @iwantanewhead

The Zoo Diaries

Frances Pauli

Part Four

Previously…

At the Rainriver Zoological Gardens, one escape became the catalyst for a series of unfortunate incidents. The tortoise, Oliver, roamed the zoo as a fugitive, searching for his missing cage mate, Miranda. When the Zoo-cam caught him interacting with the elephant, zoo attendance spiked, putting more pressure on the animals inside and increasing crowd-related stress but inspiring a zoo-wide photography contest which drove the crowds to push their limits, tossing trash into the animal enclosures, and crossing fences that were meant for their protection. Oliver was led to the aviary, but his pigeon guide betrayed him and, once he'd gotten her inside, left him to be recaptured.

Determined to escape again, Oliver made a deal with the devil. The crow, Debra, promised to lead him to Miranda. A well-meaning keeper supplied Gonzo with chocolate-covered coffee beans, and Charlie the lion dreamed of his true nature, haunted by the aroma of the crowds' hot dogs.

RAINRIVER ZOOLOGICAL PARK

TO ALL EMPLOYEES
WITH THE SUCCESS OF OUR FIRST EVER VIDEO AND PHOTOGRAPH CONTEST, ATTENDANCE NUMBERS HAVE NOW REACHED RECORD HIGHS. WE REALIZE THIS HAS INCREASED BOTH WORKLOADS AND STRESS LEVELS, AND THAT THE UNPRECEDENTED CROWDS ARE CAUSING MINOR, DAY-TO-DAY DIFFICULTIES AROUND ZOO GROUNDS.
WE THANK EACH AND EVERY ONE OF YOU FOR YOUR HARD WORK AND

EXTRA EFFORT DURING THIS WONDERFUL BUT STRESSFUL TIME.

WE ALSO ASK THAT YOU JOIN US IN WELCOMING OUR NEW SECURITY STAFF, A NECESSARY AND VITAL ADDITION TO THE RAINRIVER TEAM. WE ARE CONFIDENT THEY WILL BE OF GREAT ASSISTANCE IN KEEPING ZOO OPERATIONS FULLY FUNCTIONAL AND SAFE FOR ALL INVOLVED.

IN ORDER TO ASSIST THEM IN THAT EFFORT, WE REMIND YOU ALL TO BE VIGILANT AND REPORT ANY ISSUES. MAKE SURE ALL ZOO SIGNAGE IS VISIBLE AND REPORT ANY INFRACTIONS TO SECURITY IMMEDIATELY. IF WE ALL PULL TOGETHER, WE CAN ADAPT TO THIS NEW INFLUX OF VISITORS WITH AS FEW DIFFICULTIES AS POSSIBLE.

WE APPRECIATE YOUR EXTRA EFFORTS AND INVITE YOU TO SAVE THE DATE FOR OUR UPCOMING EMPLOYEE APPRECIATION POTLUCK BAR-B-QUE. SIGN-UPS CAN BE FOUND IN THE EMPLOYEE BREAK ROOM.

—MANAGEMENT

The Crow

Debra watches them dart the grizzly. She knows the gun is not lethal, that the dart's poison will not kill the bear, but when he shudders and flops onto his side, her feathers prickle in delight.

It would be like that, she thinks, if he were hit with a real bullet.

She has lighted on the tall stump that is a broken-off tree, a casualty to some long-ago storm. When it fell, it lay across the trench and nearly let the bear escape. He might have, she remembers. He could have climbed that fortunate bridge right to freedom.

He could have eaten someone.

But the stupid bear ignored the opportunity. Conditioned to his captivity, he stayed in his cage, and men with grumbling, noisy saws quickly broke the ramp to bits and carried them away.

Only the jagged stump remains, and Debra perches there while They-who-shoot-guns roll the sleeping Grizzly onto a tarp.

He is too heavy for them, too big. It takes four just to rock him back and forth. Each time, the shaggy pelt ripples. The bear rolls right back to the position in which he began.

They-who-shoot-guns curse and argue among themselves. They sound like crows, like a murder of their own. Debra approves of this chaos. She imagines Hector will wake soon and eat one of them.

But the bear sleeps on. He is dead weight, but eventually they heave him into position. They drag him, in the flimsy tarp, all the way to a very clever door.

Debra approves of this, too. The clever door is a trick, and she adores trickery. It stands beside the small square den opening, and it has been painted to match the rock around it. It is not smooth either. If she hadn't been a very clever crow, she might even have been surprised when it opened.

Her sharp caw is only a cry of triumph. An appreciation of a very clever trick. When she tells the story to the rest of the zoo, she will remember that detail the most.

They shot the bear. They dragged him through a very clever door, but *I could see it there the whole time.*

Debra puffs and watches as the tarp, the bear, and They-who-shoot-guns vanish through the gap in the rock. She keeps her eyes fixed on the opening, stares as the door closes again. Stares, and is convinced she can still see it.

"You never know," she will tell them all. "You never know *where* a door might be, do you?"

Grizzly Caged

Hector wakes slowly. He is confused at first, his vision blurry. The voices around him chatter in soft, familiar tones.

For a breath, he believes he is a cub again.

The surface he sprawls on is smoother than his den, colder against his belly. He moans softly, and the cadence of the voices shift.

On reflex, Hector churrs. It is a happy sound, a song of contentment, and it has never failed to earn him the attention he craves. Even now, he hears approval.

He churrs louder, rumbling until his whole body shakes. His muscles are sore and flaccid, but he manages to sit, to blink until he can actually see them.

Bars to all sides.

They've locked him in a metal box, a tiny container for an enormous bear. Outside it, faces press all around him. They peer in, eyes shining and mouths tight. Watching him.

He makes the sound and sees the pleasure flicker from one face to the next.

They are doctors, Hector thinks. He knows them from his youth, the odd, loose-fitting skins they wear, the tiny boards they carry, marking with their pens the way the artist does but never once showing him what they work on.

Hector believes they capture his likeness just the same. They record him, too, and he tilts his head and poses.

He remembers too late that his bones were hurting, that he could barely stand to walk this morning. Now, however, the quick movement brings no pain. The doctors make their markings, and Hector tests his joints. He twists and reaches and finds no agony.

This pleases them, too, and he adds more churring for good measure. He *performs* for them, and he remembers They-who-cared.

His brother is not here.

He is too old to wrestle anyway.

Hector sits in a metal box, watched and captured, and is happy for the first time in forever.

Lion Enclosure

Someone drops a cell phone into Charlie's cage. It is inevitable, really, with the jostling and shoving, the sheer number of devices. The black rectangle flips end over end, arches out, and falls, unerringly, on the lion's side of the trench.

Charlie sees it land. He has been lying in the sun, thinking of the veldt dream, and is not really interested until he smells the squeaky meat.

His lioness has already gone to investigate, but Charlie huffs, slashes his tail and approaches on the tips of his paws. His strutting drives her off, but she grumbles, mouthing back at him as she stalks away.

The phone lies in the long grass beside the trench wire. Charlie knows this is electrified, that it will give a nasty shock if he is careless enough to touch it. He lowers his head and sniffs, drinks in the meaty smell which clings to the dropped phone.

He uses one paw to bat the rectangle away from the wire, teases it to a safe distance before lowering his face to the screen.

His jaws open. He huffs, tastes the air, and is carried back into the dream. His eyes close. He lets his tail lash.

His tongue stretches, swipes over a slick surface, and tastes only a disappointingly faint flavor. It is the meat. His mind pairs it with the scent, fills in around the flavor until Charlie believes he can fully taste it.

He can hear it squeaking.

He can hear it screaming.

It is too slick to bite, too solid. Like his blood ice. Charlie wedges it between his front paws and wraps his jaws around it. He breathes. He imagines.

He uses his tongue to gather the traces, to lick and lick until all he can taste is hot plastic.

Elephant Paddock

Shanti is thrilled when Oliver appears. She has been standing over his exit all evening and has been watched far too closely by They-who-carry-guns. Their continued scrutiny makes her nervous, and she is relieved when the familiar, flat face pokes free of the earth.

One tortoise fills the tunnel mouth, and Shanti finally has someone to talk to.

"Wait," she lowers her trunk to hold him in position, to keep his presence hidden. "They've only made three passes tonight."

She knows that there will be five before they leave for the evening. That two more times They-who-carry-guns will march along her chain-linked fence with their clipped steps and shining badges.

"It will be safe soon," she tells the tortoise, "But you must wait."

She thinks he understands her caution. Already, it has been two days since They-who-keep-cages-barred returned him to his enclosure. Oliver is not a rushing animal. Not like the zebras who move at the slightest sound and are impossible to count properly.

The tortoise is deliberate. He is like her.

"Tell me," Shanti swings her trunk and whispers, "why you have to escape."

So, Oliver tells her his story. He remains in his tunnel, whispering as They-who-carry-guns pass another time. He talks about his bird, Miranda, about the day she miraculously appeared in his pen and how he followed her long strides around and around until she finally spoke to him.

Shanti doesn't like this bird from the start. When Oliver describes her with his warm words, Miranda seems cold and distant. She was not a kind animal, Shanti thinks. But Oliver loves her.

They-who-carry-guns pass again, but Shanti says nothing. She lets the tortoise spill his story, and she counts the times his voice crackles. She measures the cadence of his speech patterns and calculates the odds he's about to have his heart broken.

When he gets to the part about the pigeon, Shanti flaps her ears and stamps in sympathy. When he mentions the crow, she trumpets out loud.

"Crows cannot be trusted," she says. "They always lie."

"Unless there is better sport in telling the truth," Oliver says. He has thought this through, apparently. He believes he can outsmart the devil.

Shanti hopes he can, but she realizes they have spoken for too long. They have lingered over the story and eaten up the larger half of the nighttime.

"I think it's too late to count you again," Shanti says. "But I will still bend the fence."

"No."

Oliver's answer makes her tingle. She remembers his shapes, and she hopes she is not as cold as his bird.

"I will go tomorrow," the tortoise declares. "When there is more time."

"I'm sorry," Shanti says. She has let him linger over his story for her own pleasure. She is as bad as a crow.

But Oliver's voice seems brighter. He speaks with less crackling now. "It was good to talk," he says. "Good to share it all with someone else."

Shanti is thrilled. She scuffs her big feet and looks at the sky. One star. One tortoise.

"It's not daylight yet," Oliver says. "If you'd still like to count me."

Shanti steps back, making room for him to leave his hole. She watches the shell emerge, one row of patterns at a time, and thinks she has never been happier.

Hyena Removed

They-who-bring-food drop something disgusting in Alice's cage. The smell mingles with her food, confusing her. At first, she thinks a dead cub is hidden in the fluffy blanket they've given her. She drags it to the far corner of the cage and finds nothing. Only cloth that reeks, that smells of urine and male hyena.

Alice tries to bury it, but the cage floor is not dirt. She splits three of her claws before she gives up, pushes the smelly cloth into a wad, and leaves it. She returns to her meal.

The cat watches her eat. He has taken to staring at her when he is bored, which is far too frequent for Alice's tastes. He ignores his own food, waits to acknowledge it until Alice retires to her corner for the evening.

She lies as far as possible from the nasty blanket, but already the scent is less offensive. She will ignore it, like she ignores the cat. She will let it sit, stinking in the shadows, until she can't smell it any longer.

Eventually, she will seek out the blanket. She will go to it, dig and push at the fabric, searching for any trace of the scent.

She is not in season yet, but Alice remembers the last time. She will ignore the blanket and the smell for now. But she thinks, in a few more days, the stink of it will be not nearly as offensive.

Tortoise Abroad

Oliver meets the crow outside Shanti's paddock. The bird has been waiting for him, has paced and cackled atop a picnic table while the elephant pried up her fence. Oliver emerges to the clattering of metal. He thanks his gigantic friend, taking his time while the crow frets.

He plays a slow game, a long con. He smiles when the bird's feathers prickle.

"It's going to take you a while," Debra croaks. "You should hurry."

Oliver wants to hurry. He wants to see Miranda tonight, but his stumpy legs move with careful deliberation. The crow bounces. She hops and sputters. He has not decided what she wants. Maybe, like the pigeon, she means to use him. Does Debra long for a free ticket into the marshlands?

Oliver doesn't trust the bird, but when she takes to wing, he follows. The crow lands on the sign in front of the macaque cage, waits for him. They dance their mutual deception, while the zoo watches, holds its breath.

The monkey is not asleep. He flings something that makes the bird duck and screech. Oliver enjoys her fury. He walks quicker, however, worried the assault will drive her away.

She only moves down the path, only lands on a bench beside some bushes while Oliver works his way past the ape house.

The macaque does not attack him, but Oliver hears it, whispering to itself as he passes. The words are muddled. The animal's voice is low and quick. Oliver sees it as shadow only, hunched against a wall, rocking and whispering.

Mad. The crowds and the captivity have broken the primate, and Oliver is glad when his feet carry him beyond that cage. Relief floods his shell when the crow leads him on again, right at a place where the pathways branch. Left where they make a Y around the nocturnal house.

They pass a cement ring where the sound of water lapping against the walls echoes skyward. Here the crow pauses, perches atop the basin walls, and calls taunts to the denizens inside.

Oliver cannot see them, but they beep softly, throw insults back up their shaft enclosure. He imagines living inside a pit and shivers.

"Hurry," Debra caws.

Oliver slows his steps then thinks better of it in case she gets bored and abandons him. He hurries. He must see Miranda again.

"The marsh is by the family farm." The crow hops back to him, strutting across the path before his blunt nose. "If you don't make it tonight, you can hide in there."

Oliver grunts, sniffs for the lie in her words, for a warble of deceit. "What will you do?" he asks. "When we get to the marsh?"

"I have a plan to pry up the net," she says. "It's not hard. There are many stones nearby, but you may have to push the larger ones."

"I will." Oliver thinks she needs him to get inside, but the crow shakes herself and flutters a few steps ahead.

"It is damp in there," she says. "You won't like it."

"Will you?" He pauses, watches her smooth again.

"No." The crow's eye is a clear-bright gem, a steady beacon. "I won't go in there. After the net, you're on your own."

Oliver thinks she lies, but her steady gaze haunts him after she delivers him to the family farm. After she has found him an empty stall to hide in. Long after she has covered him with straw and left him for the day.

He waits, surrounded by the farm animals, by tall guests and shrieking children. He thinks he must guess what trick she will play on him, and he thinks about it for long hours. He hides, warm and secure, and believes he will not be a fool again.

Ape House

Gonzo has not slept. His head feels swollen, full of cottony down. He smacks his lips again and again, rubbing his face with both leathery palms. He shivers, but he is not cold. It is as if he has been in ice too long, can no longer feel it. His limbs quake, and he closes his eyes against even the softest sounds.

The troop waking is a parade of gongs and trumpets. Their nails scratch at the hard floor. Their yawns are deafening.

Gonzo hunches, holds his head, and cries aloud when they rattle the bars inside.

He drags himself back through the square door. Perhaps water will help. But when he limps to the rubber basin and dunks his face, the relief is only cursory. He drinks. He shivers. He needs the bean again.

The troop cavorts, and Gonzo leaps at them, baring his teeth and slapping whoever is slow enough, unlucky enough to remain in range. He gives them his teeth, spins, and gnashes until they all abandon him.

They scamper out into the light, and he drags himself to the bars and the aisle.

He checks the ledge, but there are no crumbs left. He searches the straw, but the black cherries had no real skin, melted in his mouth so that he finds no trace of them.

When They-who-bring-food arrive, Gonzo sits, glaring into the aisle. He-who-sweeps is with them. He slumps over his broom, but Gonzo catches him looking back. He is a sneaky primate, curled and glancing sideways.

Gonzo fears he has been punished for giving him the bean, but when the troop returns, when They-who-feed bring breakfast and move on with their tubs, a miracle occurs.

The troop dives on the fruit and biscuits. Their noises drill into Gonzo's skull, but his eyes stick to He-who-sweeps. The broom still brushes at the aisle, but it is creeping toward the macaque enclosure.

He-who-sweeps digs one paw into his coverall pocket. He whistles a note that nearly cracks Gonzo, that is so high and so lingering that the monkey has to close his eyes. When he opens them, He-who-sweeps is near. The pocket paw emerges as a fist. The fist flashes to the ledge, opens, flies back to the broom while Gonzo seizes a fresh paw-full of dark beans.

The stars align and the monkey stuffs his lips with his addiction.

X-RAY

RAINRIVER ZOOLOGICAL GARDENS
VETERINARY RECORD

URSUS HORRIBILIS
    MALE
    AGE 19

X-RAY RESULTS:
    BONE SPURS
    HAIRLINE FRACTURES OVER
    SKELETAL STRUCTURE
    SWELLING IN HIP REGION

MUSCULATURE: GOOD
    EYES: GOOD
    HEARING: GOOD
    HEARTRATE: NORMAL

DIAGNOSIS:
    ADVANCED STAGE ARTHRITIS

TREATMENT:
    PAIN REDUCER DAILY BY BODY
    WEIGHT IN FOOD OR BY
    INJECTION

Grizzly Caged

Hector stuffs his paw through the bars and wiggles it, palm pads up, until She-who-takes-notes drops a grape onto it. He curls his claws around the fruit, brings it inside the box and lips it more slowly than necessary.

The clipboard rattles as she writes. She is not an artist, but as a substitute, he thinks she does all right. When he churrs and tilts his head to one side, her mouth curls upwards in pleasure.

Hector has suffered three injections, needles stabbed through his bars on long sticks. Piercing jabs, they poke through his thick skin and make him wince. There is no way to avoid these. His metal box allows him little movement.

Though the shots are painful, his bones no longer ache. He understands that the doctors have done this, and he churrs and sits as upright as he can for them.

At first, She-who-takes-notes fed him tidbits from a similar stick. Hector has charmed her, however, and when his paw comes out again, she is quick with another grape. She no longer flinches from him. She smiles, and the bear brattles like an engine sputtering.

On the wall behind her, a picture of his bones hangs. Hector thinks it is not art. Photos are beneath him, after all. But there is something appealing about the way the light shines through his ghostly outline. There is something seductive here. Something that reminds him of the early days with his brother.

He churrs, reaches, and stuffs down grapes until She-who-takes-notes is forced to put down her clipboard and focus fully on the bear.

Elephant Paddock

Shanti counts her straw. Her trunk curls against her forehead, careful not to blow away the frail bundles. She has gathered them into groups of ten to make the counting simpler. There is no wind, and the damned crows have moved on with Oliver's most recent departure.

The elephant lines up three-hundred bits of straw in three rows of ten bundles each. She has counted her tortoise friend three times, helped him find freedom twice.

She flutters her ears. Her scrub tail flicks against her saggy buttocks. Satisfied. She sighs as she counts, certain that she has helped, that somewhere Oliver carries his 37 hexagonal scute patterns toward victory.

Shanti counts as her paddock rail fills with gaping faces. She imagines them, as they pack together, as plates on an enormous domed tortoise shell.

She does not know she is in love. Shanti only sees the perfectly aligned shapes, one against the next. She only feels a fluttering in her belly, a warm contentment as she counts her straw, thinking of Oliver. Thinking he will want to return eventually, and that there was no reason to let her count him so many times... and yet he did.

Her trunk tightens at the thought of seeing him again, and she lays her bits and bundles into looser groups, rounding the lines until they make a high arc, a gentle dome for her to count again.

The Crow

Debra inspects the net while the tortoise sleeps. She has stashed him in the family farm where, even if discovered, his presence is unlikely to cause an alert. All the souls penned in that area of the zoo are subject to interaction, are forced to wander the paddocks while the crowd's offspring molest them.

She is certain Oliver will be fine there, and she is just as sure that she is clever enough to find a way to trap him inside the marsh.

The bottom of the netting is weighted, staked to the earth at regular intervals to prevent anything larger than a vole from digging beneath it. It is these diminutive rodents, however, who have shown her the way in. For their crisscrossed tunneling has loosened a stake or two. There are now places where the net gaps and moves, and a very clever bird ought to be able to hike it upwards.

At least high enough to admit one tortoise.

Debra cackles and struts along the perimeter. There are six stakes missing now, a few others that are loose and easy to pull. She examines each breach and its surroundings and picks a site where the path nearby curves around a bronze statue of a heron. Flat stones surround its base, and Debra thinks they will be perfect.

She believes she should let the tortoise move them, that there is glorious sport in Oliver constructing his own trap. But time concerns her.

She decides to help a little, to be certain they can get him in before they are caught in the act of building.

The crow chuckles, flaps to the statue, and eyes the stones. The largest ones, the tortoise will have to shove. She selects a few that are smaller, flat smooth stones she believes will stack easily. Then, one by one, she plucks them from their arrangement and carries them to the marshland netting.

One by one, she lays them where they will be close at hand. When the time comes to trick the tortoise, Debra wants to be front and center. She wants to see the net fall, witness the dawning realization that he has been caught by a trap of his own making. That he is imprisoned inside with his own misery.

Lion Enclosure

There is a rain of debris into the lions' enclosure. Ever since Charlie's encounter with the cellular phone, more things are dropped, flung even, into his range.

They-who-carry-guns frequent the Savannah more regularly, policing the rail, but only managing to pause the tide of offenses piling up on both sides of the trench and its hot wire. There are too many people, and the guns, it seems, do not fire.

Charlie huffs. He has taken to lounging much closer to the debris field, guarding the offerings like the king he is. Those that interest him are quickly pounced upon. He has tasted many new things.

Popcorn. Soft animals filled with white fluff. Leather straps, little square cameras, lattes, and many more phones. He ignores these now, though he still enjoys shredding the fuzzy toy animals. He appreciates the buttery taste of popcorn, too, and he chews the leather bits out of boredom.

But mostly, Charlie waits for the squeaky meat.

When the crowd tosses him these, the long reddish tubes of meat, Charlie roars and pounces. He snarls in case the lionesses dare to sneak closer, and he bites. He chews and devours with all the gusto of a natural predator.

It is delicious, somehow feeling both raw and wholly artificial. The hot dogs hold traces of his minced diet, but along with that they carry a thousand new flavors, unrecognized tastes that drive straight from Charlie's tongue to his brain.

He is rabid for it.

He chews and dreams, and in the night his veldt is peopled with hot dog monsters that sing to him from the far shadows. He can smell them there, always out of reach. And when he wakes, there are even more faces, more paws to toss him offerings.

Charlie basks in his fame, eats his hot dogs, and thinks there will never be enough to satiate him.

Tortoise Abroad

Oliver struggles free of the straw. He cannot shake himself, hasn't the flexibility to do more than swipe a forefoot across his face to clear his vision. Bits of the pale hay poke into the gaps in his shell, forward and back.

He is prickled, and the soft skin folds around his neck and legs begin to itch.

The crow goads him onward. She bounces along the stall railing until Oliver picks up his pace. Night has fallen, and Debra becomes a set of dancing eyes in the darkness. A gleaming beak like a knife slash as she calls his name.

Oliver moves to her command, but he is thinking, thinking that her urgency cannot bode well for him.

"It's ready. It's ready," she sings while bobbing.

Oliver smells the trap, but his brain fills with Miranda. He shuffles eagerly from the family farm and follows the bouncing crow. The straw pokes him with each step, but eventually it falls free or he forgets to care about it.

Debra leads him down the pathway. Just beyond the family farm she perches on a miraculous thing. It is enormous and made of metal, but its shape is Miranda's shape. Oliver gazes up at it and shivers.

The statue guards the marshland, and Oliver thinks it is an omen. He believes the crow now. His love is inside the nets.

Debra has gathered a pile of small stones. She shows him her work. She explains her plan, and Oliver waves his long neck from side to side. It is a good idea, clever, and though he knows he will have to go carefully, to watch for deception along the way, his heart races.

Debra lifts the net, only a fraction at first. She is a small thing, made of hollow bones and not strong. Oliver shoves the smallest rock into the gap. They repeat this maneuver twice before there is enough room for him to push the tip of a foot underneath.

He watches the crow stack a third rock on top of the other two, lifting the net one inch higher. If she means to dart inside, to leave him like a dirty pigeon, this is her opportunity.

But Debra bounces backwards and eyes the widening gap instead.

"A large one next," she croaks. "One to hold it up while we remove these."

Oliver decides her game is not to steal his entrance. She really means to get him inside, to whatever end, and that knowing moves his feet much faster.

He wobbles to the statue and finds a large stone, bulldozes it, rolls it with his flat nose onto the path and back to their building site.

The net rises, one stone at a time, each larger than the last until it is half his height and there are no larger rocks to be found. Then, Debra begins to stack again. She places small stones atop the big one while Oliver wedges his neck beneath the net. He lifts his head, uses his body as a lever to pry the material higher.

It resists them. They have reached the limits of the next stake down and now it fights against their effort.

Oliver stares at it, frantic and half tangled. The lower edge has caught on his shell lip, but he is halfway through. He is stepping inside the boundary now, pulling while the crow screams at him.

Her claws scratch at his dome. She rides him as Peg did, and Oliver thrashes in panic before her words settle.

"Wait, idiot. You're stuck."

He is frantic. He is trapped. He will knock her free if he has to.

But when he pauses to decide, the crow bobs down, uses her beak to lift the net from his rim. She pulls it, and with a deep twang, it slides free, resting atop his dome with her and, when Oliver presses forward, slipping up and over.

The crow is swept from his shell. The net passes freely over his body.

Oliver surges ahead and walks into the marshland. He steps on grass and soggy earth. His body rocks from one side to the other, and the net falls away behind him, snapping back to the ground and leaving the crow outside after all.

They have done it. Oliver's heart bounces now. He is inside.

The crow's plan, *their* plan, has worked.

Copyright

Title information

Metaphorosis April 2023

ISSN: 2573-136X (online)
ISBN: 978-1-64076-255-8 (e-book)
ISBN: 978-1-64076-256-5 (paperback)

Copyright

Works of fiction

This book contains works of fiction. Characters, dialogue, places, organizations, incidents, and events portrayed in the works are fictional and are products of the author's imagination or used fictitiously. Any resemblance to actual persons, places, organizations, or events is coincidental.

All rights reserved

Moral rights asserted

Each author whose work is included in this book has asserted their moral rights, including the right to be identified as the author of their respective work(s).

Publisher

Metaphorosis Magazine is an imprint of Metaphorosis Publishing
Neskowin, OR, USA

www.metaphorosis.com

"Metaphorosis" is a registered trademark.

Discounts available

Substantial discounts are available for educational institutions, including writing workshops. Discounts are also available for quantity purchases. For details, contact Metaphorosis at metaphorosis.com/about

Metaphorosis Publishing

Metaphorosis offers beautifully written science fiction and fantasy. Our imprints include:

Metaphorosis Magazine
Plant Based Press
Verdage
Vestige

You can also find us:
@MetaphorosisMag, @Metaphorosis
www.facebook.com/metaphorosis

Help keep Metaphorosis running by supporting us at
Patreon.com/metaphorosis

See more about some of our books on the following pages.

Metaphorosis Magazine

Metaphorosis

a magazine of speculative fiction

Metaphorosis is an online speculative fiction magazine dedicated to quality writing. We publish an original story every week, along with author bios, interviews, and notes on story origins.

We also publish monthly print and e-book issues, as well as yearly Best of and Complete anthologies.

Come and see us online at magazine.Metaphorosis.com.

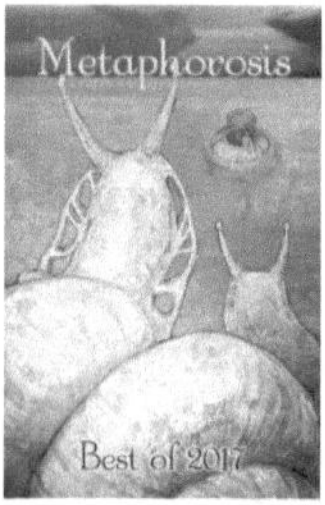

Plant Based Press

Vegan-friendly science fiction and fantasy, including anthologies of the year's best SFF stories, from 2016-2020.

Chambers of the
Heart

*speculative stories
by
B. Morris Allen*

A heart that's a building, a dog that's a program, a woman sinking irretrievably — stories about love, loss, and motion.

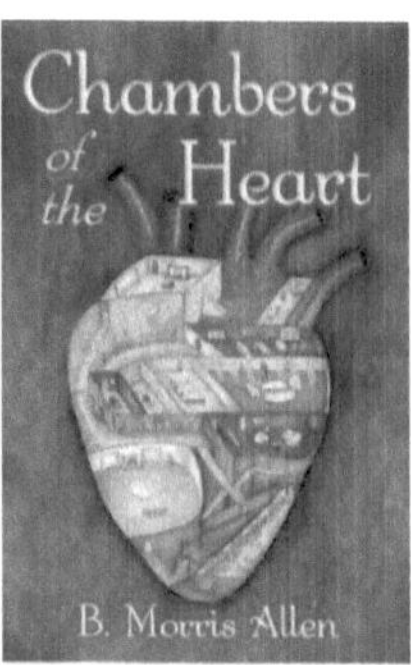

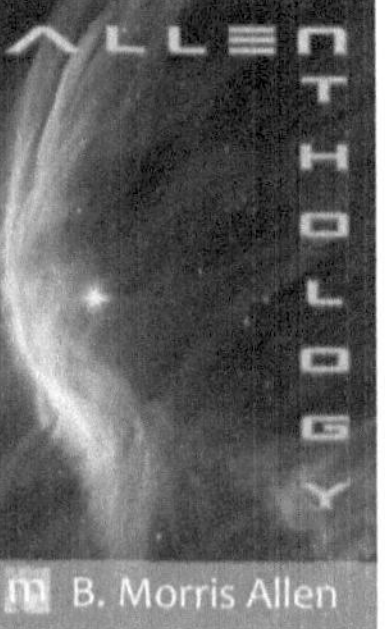

Susurrus

A darkly romantic story of magic, love, and suffering.

Allenthology:
Volume I

Including three full collections of SFF stories.

Verdage

Science fiction and fantasy books for writers — full of great stories, often with an additional focus on the craft of speculative fiction writing.

Reading 5X5 x3

Changes

How do stories move from 'maybe' to published?

Here are 15 case studies of stories published in *Metaphorosis* magazine.

Reading 5X5 x2

Duets

How do authors' voices change when they collaborate?

A round-robin of five talented science fiction and fantasy authors collaborating with each other and writing solo.

Including stories by Evan Marcroft, David Gallay, J. Tynan Burke, L'Erin Ogle, and Douglas Anstruther.

Score

an SFF symphony

An anthology with an emotional score from the heights of joy to the depths of despair – but always with a little hope shining through.

Reading 5X5

Five stories, five times

See how different writers take on the same material.

Reading 5X5

Writers' Edition

Two extra stories, the story seed, and authors' notes on writing.

Vestige

Novelettes, novellas, and novels by Metaphorosis authors.

The Nocturnals
Mariah Montoya

Night is Dangerous.
Day is deadly.

Where day and night last thirty years, humans move constantly stay ahead of the night and cruel Nocturnals that call it home. But a boy is lost out there.

www.ingramcontent.com/pod-product-compliance
Lightning Source LLC
Chambersburg PA
CBHW030431120726
47903CB00003B/915